Red Sky in the Morning

Elizabeth Laird

MACMILLAN CHILDREN'S BOOKS

First published 1988 byWilliam Heinemann Limited
Published 2006 by Macmillan Children's Books

This edition published 2016 by Macmillan Children's Books
an imprint of Pan Macmillan
20 New Wharf Road, London N1 9RR
Associated companies throughout the world
www.panmacmillan.com

ISBN 978-1-5098-0293-7

5 7 9 8 6 4

A CIP catalogue record for this book is available from
the British Library.

Printed and bound by CPI Group (UK) Ltd, Croydon CR0 4YY

Red Sky in the Morning

Elizabeth Laird is the multi-award-winning author of several much-loved children's books. She has been shortlisted for the prestigious Carnegie Medal six times. She lives in Britain now, but still likes to travel as much as she can.

*Books by Elizabeth Laird published
by Macmillan Children's Books*

For Graham, Margaret and Janet

Preface

I was four years old when my little brother Alistair was born. I can remember the first time I saw him, lying in a cot by my mother's bed, thin wisps of hair on his large head. I lifted the corner of his coverlet and saw his little feet. I was amazed that feet could be so tiny.

I was too young to understand Alistair's many disabilities, or what it might feel like to be him, but I knew how to make him laugh, by pushing my face up against the bars of his cot and sticking my tongue out, or dancing around and waving the skirt of my dress. I knew how to make him cry too, and I regret to say that I did that sometimes, when I felt jealous of all the attention he was getting.

People often ask me if I put real people into my stories. The answer is no. I might borrow a bit here and there — the way someone speaks, or a particular little habit, or a real incident that I remember. But my characters are themselves, made up, with lives of their own. The family in *Red Sky in the Morning* is nothing like my family, and I don't think that either Anna or Katy is much like me. They're just themselves.

But there's one exception to my usual rule. The character of Ben in this book is my brother Alistair.

Chapter One

As long as I live, I shall never forget the night my brother was born. For one thing, I didn't get a wink of sleep. I'd only been in bed a few minutes when I heard Dad talking on the telephone. My bedroom's pretty small, and if I lean out of bed far enough I can open the door without actually getting out of bed, so I did, and I heard Dad say,

'That's right, the second house on the left past the shops. And please hurry.'

His voice sounded so urgent I guessed at once he must be calling the ambulance and I knew my time had come. Well, it was Mum's time really, but mine too, in a way, because I was going to be in charge while she was away. I'd practised everything in my mind, so I just got calmly out of bed, and put on my dressing gown, and groped around for my glasses. Then I went calmly out of the room and walked down the hall to Mum and Dad's bedroom. I didn't even run.

'Now just relax, Mum,' I said. 'Everything's under control.' I must have said it too calmly because no one took any notice. Mum's face was screwed up, and Dad was looking at her, standing quite still, with one leg in his trousers and the other out. He looked perfectly ridiculous. Then Mum's face went ordinary again, and she turned her head and saw me, and she looked quite normal. In fact, she gave me a smile. Then Dad started pulling on his trousers again. It was like starting up a video again after a freeze frame.

After that, everything I'd planned to say was swept out of my head, because things happened too fast. Mum's face screwed up again, and she started taking loud, rasping breaths. I've never seen such an awful look in anyone's eyes, not even in a war film.

Dad grabbed his jacket, and pushed past me out of the room. Then I suppose he must have realized it was me, because he came back and ruffled my hair the way he does when he wants to be nice to me. I hate it, but I don't like hurting his feelings, so I just suffer in silence.

'Be a nice girl,' he said. 'Go and get me a cup of tea. The ambulance won't be here for another five minutes. I've got to go and phone your granny.'

I couldn't believe it. I've never heard anything so callous in all my life. There was his wife, probably dying, in the most awful agony, trying to give birth to his own child, and all he could think of were his own selfish pleasures. I realized how woman has suffered from man's selfishness since time began.

'Sorry, Dad,' I said with dignity. 'I expect Mum needs me. You'll find the tea in the usual place.'

But then Mum gave an awful scream, and Dad rushed back into the bedroom and shut the door in my face. I didn't dare go in. I didn't even want to any more. I felt too small and helpless. Frightful thoughts rushed through my mind, like what would happen if Mum died, and I had to sacrifice my youth to looking after Dad and bringing up Katy, who was seven, and absolutely horrible.

The minute I thought of Katy, I remembered my responsibilities. It was my job to run the house and family while Mum was otherwise engaged, and I decided I had better start by running Katy. I went back down the corridor to her room.

Katy is an unusually irritating child. Even Mum admits that she's a nuisance. She says it's because Katy's going through a stage, but either Mum's wrong, or else it's a very long stage, because Katy

seems to have been in it since she was born. One
of the worst things about her is that you can never
get her to go to sleep. We all have to creep around
the house once she's gone to bed, and I can't even
play my own tapes in my own room, which I feel,
quite frankly, is a violation of my human rights. And
she wakes up in the middle of the night if a moth
so much as brushes its wings against her bedroom
window. I never would have thought she'd sleep
through the noise Mum was making, but that's the
maddening thing about Katy. She's so unpredictable.
There wasn't a sound coming from her room. I
knelt down, and looked through the keyhole. She
always has a nightlight on because she thinks she's so
delicious that witches are just dying to come and eat
her in the night, so I could see clearly enough that
she was fast asleep.

'Well,' I thought, 'that gives me one less thing to
worry about,' but at the same time I almost wished
Katy had been awake, because I hadn't got anything
to do. I certainly wasn't intending to betray Mum by
making Dad a cup of tea.

Then I realized that I could at least phone Granny,
which Dad seemed to have forgotten about, so I
went downstairs to the phone in the hall, and was

just beginning to dial when the front doorbell went. The ambulance had come.

There were only two ambulancemen but they filled up our small downstairs hall completely. It's so narrow that if two people meet, one of them has to turn sideways and stand against the wall while the other squashes past. I used to think of ways of making sure it wasn't me who had to stand against the wall, like pretending, if I was holding something, that it was very heavy, or being in a hurry for the loo, but I stopped all that kind of childish thing years ago. Still, I've never stopped minding that our hall is so mean and small, not like Debbie's (she used to be my best friend), and suddenly I got worried about it.

How would they get Mum down the stairs on a stretcher? Supposing it stuck, like that time when Dad was fitting units in their bedroom, and he and Mum were trying to get the old wardrobe down the stairs? It got completely wedged between the wall and the banisters, and Dad had to get a saw and cut it in half before it took off any more wallpaper. He was furious, and it took hours to free the wardrobe. But Mum hadn't got hours. If she got stuck on her stretcher, she'd have to have the baby right there on the stairs.

As it happened, Mum didn't need a stretcher at all. Dad came out of the bedroom, looking pale and shaky and awful, and the men ran upstairs, and then one rushed out again and said,

'Where's the telephone, love?'

And he dialled, and when I heard him talking I started to feel trembly myself, and sick.

'This is Alan here,' he said. 'I've got an emergency over on Blythe Road. Lady in labour. Too far gone to get her to hospital. She's started pushing, and the baby's almost there. Stan's doing what he can, but he says it's not looking quite right. Best get a doctor over here quick. We've got the oxygen and stuff, but we haven't got all the neo-natal kit if they need to do full resuscitation.'

He must have forgotten about me, because he started off up the stairs again when he'd put the receiver down. I couldn't bear to let him go. I had to know what was going on.

'Is — is everything all right?' I said. It sounded more feeble than it meant to, but I didn't know what to say. I was frightened.

'Course it is,' he said. He was using that awful cheerful voice they use to children when they want to deceive them. 'Just a precaution. Your mummy's going to be fine. So's the baby, I expect. It all happened just a bit too quick, that's all.'

He patted my shoulder just as if he'd been a relative. I was only twelve then, but I was mature for my age, and it was not surprising that I felt offended.

'I'm quite prepared to give blood, if necessary,' I said. The idea made me feel sick, but if Mum needed my blood, there was naturally no more to be said. He had the cheek to laugh.

'Oh, we won't need your blood,' he said. 'Best thing you can do is be a good girl and keep out of the way. Tell you what, do you know how to make a cup? Why don't you put the kettle on, then? Me and Stan could do with a cuppa when we've finished with this lot.'

If he hadn't put it like that, of course, I wouldn't have dreamed of making a cup of tea. But I knew that if I didn't he'd think I didn't know how to, so I went to the kitchen, and filled up the kettle. But all the time it was boiling, and while I was putting mugs and milk and sugar on to the tray, I kept thinking about Mum and the baby.

Up until then, I hadn't thought about the baby much as a real person. Quite honestly, I'd been shocked when Mum told me she was pregnant. I couldn't imagine her and Dad having sex. The whole idea seemed disgusting. Especially in our house. Their bedroom didn't look right for it. It was too ordinary. But I'd got used to her getting bigger, and being tired, and relying on me more for things. In some ways I'd enjoyed it. I got quite good at doing a fry-up for supper, and heating up pizzas in the oven. I could even do lamb chops and two veg, though it took hours to peel the potatoes.

Somehow, though, I hadn't thought much about the baby. I'd wanted a brother, I knew that much, mainly because I didn't want another Katy round the place, and I'd started knitting a cardigan, but I'm not much good at knitting, so I'd pulled it undone and tried to learn to crochet instead. But it got in a tangle, so I never managed to get anything finished. Dad had got the pram down out of the attic, and Mum had lined the cot again in some new flowery material. It looked pretty, waiting there all clean and empty, beside her bed, but I hadn't been able to imagine a real, live baby in it.

Then I remembered something I'd read about in a Victorian novel. Grandma's got a whole stack of them, that she used to read about a hundred and fifty years ago. They have titles like *Lost in London*, and

Little Faith, and they're all horribly sad and religious. The children go around bare foot in the snow, selling matches, and their mothers are gin-sodden, and the babies die, and when you read them you cry and cry. I even got sinusitis once, because I cried so much over *Christie's Old Organ*. But I like them too. After I've read one, I feel pure, and refined, and ready to face death.

Anyway, when babies are born in those old books, the mother's poor eldest daughter is always sent to the kitchens to boil gallons of water. It never explained what the water was for, but I knew that was the right thing to do. So I got out the pressure cooker, and the biggest pans I could find, and filled them up, and turned on every burner on the stove. I slopped a bit on the floor, but I managed all right.

It took quite a long time, finding everything, and filling them up, and I was still at work when Dr Randall came. He went up the stairs two at a time, and then another ambulance came, and the men took this funny box thing upstairs. After a while they came down again, holding it carefully, and drove away. The doctor was still there. I could hear him in Mum and Dad's bedroom, which is right above the kitchen. But the rest of the house was quiet. Then I realized that the first ambulancemen, Alan and Stan, had gone too, and they hadn't even bothered to have their cup of tea. I knew then for certain that they'd just been humouring me, and trying to keep me out of the way. Typical!

It was so quiet upstairs that I began to feel a bit worried. What could they all be doing? Was Mum all right? And shouldn't the baby be crying? Mum had promised that I'd be the first after Dad to see it, but no one had called me. I wanted desperately to know what was going on. But I felt too scared to go up and open the bedroom door and just walk in. Medical things seem kind of holy to me. Bursting in on the doctor doing something would be as bad as jumping up in church and shouting 'Hi there!' to the vicar.

Then I remembered the tea. Surely everyone would really and truly want a cup of tea by this time. After all, it was practically morning. The kitchen window was filling with a sort of greyish light, and there were red streaks across the sky. I'd never seen the dawn before. It was eerie and grand. Suitable for a birth, really. I checked that I'd put out enough mugs, filled the teapot (the kettle had boiled ages ago) and staggered upstairs with the tray. Then I put it down, and opened the door a crack, and picked it up, and went in, holding the tray in front of me so it would be the first thing they all saw.

I could see at once that they'd been having a very deep conversation. Mum was lying back in bed, looking white and tired, and Dad was sitting beside her, holding one of her hands. Dr Randall was on the other side of the bed, looking serious. Mum saw me first.

'Oh Annie!' she said, and gave a wobbly kind of laugh, and then Dad jumped up and came towards me, and made a big fuss about taking the tray. I wasn't fooled. I knew he was trying to stop me seeing Mum cry. I knew quite well that that was what she was doing.

'Where is it? Is it a boy? Can't I see him yet?' I whispered to Dad. He just stood there, not saying anything. Then he turned, with the tray in his hands, and looked over to Dr Randall, and Dr Randall came towards me and said in that stupid voice they never use to each other,

'Yes, Anna, you've got a dear little brother, but he's not very well, and we've had to take him to hospital.'

'That box,' I whispered. Somehow I couldn't

bring myself to speak normally. 'He was in that box, wasn't he? Is he . . .?'

Dr Randall smiled for the first time.

'No, he's not dead, Anna. That was only an incubator. It's a special box for babies that need extra warmth and attention. He's not going to die. But . . .'

Now it was his turn to stop and look at Dad, and this time Dad was great. He just put his hands on my shoulders.

'Your brother's not quite right,' he said. 'Dr Randall thinks he may be disabled. We won't be able to tell yet, for a week or two, but it doesn't look . . .' and then the worst possible thing happened. Dad actually cried. He didn't sob or anything. He just crumpled up a bit. That set me off, of course. I've never been able not to cry if someone else is. It's infectious, like giggling, or yawning or something. And then Mum started, and we were all crying, and I felt really sad, but one horrible part of me was looking on from outside, and thinking,

'Well, well. Fancy Mum and Dad and me all crying together over a serious family matter, and Katy still being asleep. That makes me feel really one of them.'

I still couldn't imagine the baby. I knew with my brain that it was sad, him being disabled, but I couldn't really feel it, if you know what I mean.

It's funny how you feel when you stop crying, if you've been crying with someone else. It's embarrassing of course, but quite comfortable too, in a way. You feel loving, and close together, and empty, too.

After a bit, I began to think awful thoughts. What did disabled mean? Would he look funny? Would his legs and arms jerk a lot? Somehow, because we'd all been crying together, I felt especially daring, so I came right out with it to Dr Randall.

'What do you mean, disabled?' I said.

Dr Randall shook his head.

'I was just telling your parents, Anna,' he said. 'We don't know yet. We'll have to wait and see.'

'Yes, but will he be blind, or deaf?' I asked.

Mum and Dad were sitting in a specially still kind of way, and I knew they were dying for the answer too. Dr Randall looked more cheerful.

'Oh no, I'm sure he'll be able to see and hear all right,' he said.

'Will he look nice, or will he look funny, and dribble and all that?' I asked. It sounds awful, but I cared about that more than anything.

'I don't know, Anna,' Dr Randall said. 'I honestly don't know. But all babies are very sweet, you know, even when they're . . .' he stopped.

'Can't you even tell us,' I said, 'if he'll be able to play, and go to school, and talk, and laugh, and everything?'

The cheerful look wiped itself off Dr Randall's face.

'He'll be able to laugh,' he said slowly. 'Oh yes, I'm sure he'll laugh. But for the rest, let's wait and see, shall we? I think we all need some sleep now.' He patted Mum's hand.

'You should try to rest,' he said. 'I'm sure you're very tired. You've done well to manage a home delivery with a birth of this kind. Quite unusual, in fact. I've given you a good strong dose. Make the most of it. You can phone the hospital any time, but there won't be any news until tomorrow morning. The nurse will be here to sort you out at breakfast time. And try not to worry. He's quite stable, you know. There's no danger.'

He picked up his bag and clicked it shut. He seemed suddenly in a hurry to go. The strain, I suppose. Mum always says that emotional upsets are more exhausting than anything else. Still, he didn't have much to upset him. It wasn't *his* baby that wasn't going to run about. All in the day's work for him, I should think.

He'd only been gone half a minute when he poked his head round the door again.

'There seems to be rather a lot of steam coming out of the kitchen,' he said.

Steam! Boiling water! Of course! I'd left the four burners on full blast. I jumped up like a startled rabbit, and squeezed past Dr Randall and was in the kitchen in a flash. There was so much steam I could hardly see the cooker. Fortunately, none of the saucepans had boiled dry, but the walls were streaming with water. I felt such a fool. I was afraid they'd laugh at me. Dr Randall had never even mentioned needing any boiling water. I decided I'd try to empty all the saucepans, and clear up quickly before Dad came down and saw, and then I could say that in my excitement I'd left the kettle on. But it was too late. Dad came into the kitchen right behind me.

'Very sensible, Spanner,' he said, in a matter of fact voice. He's always calling me silly names that rhyme with 'Anna'. It drives me crazy sometimes,

especially if he forgets and does it in front of other
people. It sounds so weird. But he won't stop. He
just laughs, and says, 'You know what they say, "A
loved child has many names," so you be grateful,
Gloriana.'

I was relieved, anyway, that he didn't laugh.

'Well,' I said, 'I know boiling water is the right
thing to do when a baby's born, but quite honestly,
I don't know what it's for.'

Dad didn't seem very sure either.

'Oh, sterilizing instruments or something, I
suppose,' he said vaguely. 'Anyway, we'd better go
to bed now. There's not much of tonight left.'

But I didn't feel tired at all. Not yet, anyway. I
knew I'd feel awful the next day. But just now there
were too many things I wanted to know.

'Does it always hurt that bad?' I blurted out. I
hadn't meant to ask Dad that, but I couldn't help
myself.

'Does what hurt?' he said. I excused him for being
so thick and insensitive on the grounds that he was
an ignorant male and didn't know any better.

'Having a baby, of course,' I said. 'Mum's face,
and then the way she screamed . . .'

'You'll have to ask her,' he said. 'I wouldn't

know, would I? But Mum seems to think it's worth it. It's how you and Kate were born, after all.'

'And now you've got a son, too,' I said, and then I wished I hadn't said it, because Dad looked very sad.

'Yes,' he said. 'And now I've got a son. Come on Susanna. It's bedtime.'

Chapter Two

I felt pretty funny going to school the next morning, partly because I was completely exhausted, I suppose. Dad said I could stay at home if I liked. He'd got the week off work. But I wanted to go. One reason was to get out of the house, because there was an awfully gloomy atmosphere, and Mum cried a lot, and Dad was on the phone all the time. Katy was a pest too. She'd got it into her head to be all fluffy, and sugar sweet, and babyish, and I could have kicked her.

The other reason was that I was bursting to tell everyone at school. It's not often that I have some real news. Not like Sandra, whose older brother is in the Marines, or Miranda, who goes to masses of discos, and does things with boys. Actually, I'm not all that popular at school. I used to be best friends with Debbie, ages ago, and that was fine, because everyone likes her, so they let me into their group too.

Debbie's one of the most beautiful people I've

ever seen. She's got this wonderful deep chestnut hair, that she can flick about her face and it falls back into place, like on the shampoo ads. And she's got a long, finely chiselled nose, and perfectly even teeth, and transparent skin covered with a sort of bloom, like a peach, and huge luscious eyes that are big and brown like a spaniel's. It sounds corny, but it's true. I can gaze at Debbie for hours. It's not that I'm in love with her, or anything peculiar like that. I don't even like her any more, since she started going off with Emma, who laughs at me behind my back, and calls me a health hazard because of my acne. I just like beautiful things, that's all. I've got a strong aesthetic sense. And looking at Debbie is like looking at a perfect work of art.

Ever since I knew Mum was pregnant, I'd been planning my announcement at school, so I couldn't bear to put it off. And it was lovely. Even better than I'd hoped. Everyone was fascinated.

I told it really dramatically. Well, it was dramatic, after all. It's not every baby that's born at home because it all happened too quickly for the mother to get to hospital. And then there were two ambulances, one arriving after the other, and the doctor, and me knowing how to boil up lots of water, and the doctor telling me how sensible that was (well, it was Dad really but I cheated on that bit). They loved the bit where I saw them carrying in that little box, and my dreadful premonition that something was terribly wrong, and how I'd stood, rooted to the spot in the hall, with my hand over my pounding heart, trying to pray. And then there was the relief when Dr Randall said it was only an incubator. But somehow, I couldn't tell anyone that he might be disabled. I couldn't quite admit it to myself yet.

'I wonder what he looks like?' said Debbie. 'It's a pity you didn't even get a glimpse, Anna. I bet he's got those lovely little hands and feet that babies always have. I do love babies.'

'I bet his front teeth stick out like his big sister's do, said Emma with a nasty snigger. I ignored her. I could see she was only jealous, and afraid that Debbie might start being my friend again. And for once, Debbie took my side. I'll say this for her, when she's decided to be nice to you, she's really lovely.

'Don't be daft, Em,' she said. 'Newborn babies haven't got any teeth. Anyway, Anna's teeth are going back in now with that brace thing. I bet he's sweet, Anna. Can we pop round when he's back home and see him?'

I felt a sudden chill, like when you know you haven't done the right homework and it's got to be handed in.

'I don't know. I'll have to ask Mum,' I said. 'He's quite delicate, Dr Randall says. He's got to be protected from any possible source of infection.' I looked hard at Emma when I said that. She's more of a health hazard than me. She never stops eating sweets and the fur sticks out half an inch on her teeth.

They sort of drifted off after that. All except Vicky. She's the one in our class none of us can stand. She never gets picked for team games, and no one likes sitting next to her. I do try to be nice to Vicky, or at least, not actively nasty. I know how awful it is not to be liked. But I'm not desperate enough for a friend to go round with her. I mean, there are limits.

That evening, we had a long discussion about the baby's name. Before he was born, Dad had decided on Edward. He said it sounded strong and silent and reliable. Mum wanted James. She said she'd always promised her dad that if she ever had a son, she'd call him after his grandad. I wanted something a bit more up to date, like Jason, or Jasper.

Katy and I were in Mum's bedroom when Katy brought the subject up.

'Let's call him Sam,' she said. 'Oh please darling Mummee, plee-eese.'

She was using the same whiny voice she puts on when she wants to get a Mars bar out of someone. That child has no sense of occasion. Anyway, she only likes the name Sam because her best friend Tracey's older brother is called Sam. Katy thinks she's in love with him. In love! At seven years old! I ask you.

'I know,' I said. 'Why don't we give him four names? Princes have four names. He could be James Edward Jasper Sam, then we'd all be happy.'

'No!' said Mum, suddenly and sharply. 'Not James!'

'But I thought you said you'd promised . . .' I began, but I looked at her face, and thought better of it. I seemed to be getting into deep water without quite knowing why.

Dad came in then, with a cup of tea for Mum.

'Talking about names, are you?' he said. 'Well, I've made a decision. I'm his Dad, and I've got the last word. We're going to call him Benedict. I've looked it up. It means "Blessed".'

I saw him look at Mum, but she turned her face away.

'Benedict.' I turned it over in my mind, and began to like it. Ben. Benny. Benedict.

'Benedict what?' I said. 'What's his middle name?'

'Just Benedict,' said Dad. 'I don't think he'll need another name.'

He paused, but Mum didn't say anything.

'Well, that's decided then,' said Dad, and he took the empty tray away again.

I was at school when Mum and Dad brought Ben home from the hospital. I could tell at once that something exciting had happened when I opened the front door. I sometimes think I must have special powers. I'm probably psychic, and I'd make a great witch, or a medium or something. But I wouldn't dream of getting mixed up with all that stuff. I'm too sensible. After all, you never know what kind of horrors that sort of thing can lead to.

Actually, it might have been the smell that gave me the clue. There was a faint waft of baby on the air, that powdery, milky, soft smell that they only have for the first few months. A great wave of excitement rushed over me, and I dropped my bag and tore off my anorak and raced upstairs.

Mum was just settling him down to sleep. She looked much happier than she had for the last few days. She'd been so miserable, and snappy and weepy. I'd had a horrible feeling that she might just leave Ben at the hospital and never bring him home. I felt dreadfully afraid that she wouldn't love him. And if she didn't love Ben, perhaps she would stop loving me, too. But when I saw the tenderness on her face, I felt such relief I could have danced all round the room. I felt as if she'd been a long, long way away, and had come home again.

'Come and see him, Annie,' she said.

I sometimes wonder if I would have loved Ben quite so much if Mum hadn't shown me his feet first. She lifted up the edge of his coverlet, and I saw his tiny, perfect miniature toes, pink as shells, soft as petals. He must have felt the coverlet move, because he stretched them out and then curled them up again. I hadn't ever seen anything so beautiful in my whole life.

Then Mum put the coverlet back, and pulled down the other end, and I saw him, my little darling brother, for the first time. His eyes were shut, but his mouth was still moving. It was sucking a bit, in and out. I could see at once that something was wrong

with him. His head was far too big. The veins in it
stuck out too much, and looked too blue. But beside
each lovely little ear, a curl of hair grew outwards,
corkscrewing out from his head, perfect and silky
and fine. I put out my hand to touch.

'Can I, Mum?' I said.

'Yes, of course.' She was smiling, but in that
wobbly kind of way that meant she was nearly crying
too. She bent down, and picked his nappy off the
floor, and went off with it to the bathroom, and I
was alone with Ben.

I may have been only twelve, and short-sighted,
and spotty, but I knew how to fall in love. I fell in
love with Ben at that moment.

'I don't care how handicapped you are,' I
whispered to him. 'I love you. I'll always love you.
I'll protect you, and look after you. If anyone's
going to be mean to you, they'll have to deal with
me first.'

I bent over the cot, and kissed him. It was like
kissing a rose. He moved a bit, and I felt he'd heard
me. It was silly, of course. He couldn't possibly
understand, or know who I was, or even feel much
at his age. He didn't even have his eyes open. But I
felt as if he loved me, too.

I think the few weeks after that were the happiest of my life. I no longer cared what anyone said or did to me at school. I just lived for the moment when I could get home, race up to Mum's bedroom, pick Ben up, and gave him a huge cuddle. I hardly noticed that his big head was growing bigger and bigger, and that his poor little neck was too weak to hold it up. I was too busy fussing over his nappy, and powdering his little bottom. Mum laughed at me.

'You'll make a wonderful mother yourself, one day,' she said.

'What do you mean, one day?' I thought scornfully. 'I'd make a wonderful mother now.' Apart from breastfeeding – and I couldn't do that, of course – I felt as if I could do everything else for Ben. I could dress him, and bath him, and rock him to sleep, and take him for walks in his pram.

'I notice you're not so keen on dealing with his dirty nappies, or washing his clothes,' Mum said drily. But I knew I could do all that if I had to. In fact, I even daydreamed sometimes (I knew it was wrong, but I couldn't help it) that something had happened to Mum and Dad, and I really was in charge of Ben, all by myself. Maybe it wouldn't have been so great. Maybe I'd have got bored and lonely and worried and fed up. But for a couple of hours after school every day it was perfect.

Actually, after a while, real life asserted itself again. It wasn't that I loved Ben any less, it was just that I had other things to worry about – like exams. They're quite easygoing at my school really, but at the end of the summer term every year the whole place suddenly goes berserk. They load work on to us, and make us completely neurotic. I think it's sadistic, really, to have exams in June, when we get the only decent weather we're likely to have for the whole year. I mean, what's wrong with November, when no one's got anything better to do? I blame the teachers. I'm sure they make us do exams in June so they can have an easy time invigilating, and dreaming about the holidays they're going to have in Scarborough, or the Bahamas, or somewhere. It's all right for some.

I don't know why I mind so much about exams. They scare me stiff. I think it's dreading the moment when she reads the marks out, and everyone knows whether you're one of the worst or one of the best. And the trouble with being so scared is that it stops me learning anything. My mind goes numb. I mean, how can you do brilliantly with a numb mind? And some of the exams are completely pointless. What's the idea of an art exam? You're either a genius or you aren't. And to find out which you are, they might just as well look at the last creation you did in class. I suppose they've got what Dad calls the bureaucratic mentality.

Anyway, I worked very hard that summer, and didn't do too badly. Debbie was top in History as usual, and nearly top in Geography, but I beat her in French and English. Très bien pour moi.

Partly because of exams, and partly because of Debbie going off with Emma, I didn't have much social life that summer. I suppose though, if I'm honest with myself, the real reason was Ben. I told Mum I wanted to have him all to myself, and I didn't see why I should have to share him with anyone else, but I know that it was really because I didn't want them to see him. I think Mum realized. She didn't push me into asking anyone round anyway, not even on my birthday. Actually, she wasn't seeing some of her old friends much. I noticed she kept to the house quite a lot, and didn't go out very often. Perhaps it was just having a small baby. But I don't think it was only that.

It was quite obvious to everyone after a few months

that Ben was very badly disabled. His head was twice
as big as it should have been. 'Hydrocephalus', the
doctor called it. He said they'd be able to operate
later, to take some of the fluid out of his head, so
that it would be smaller, but it wouldn't make any
difference to the handicap. We must never hope
he'd grow up normal.

'Severe mental and physical disability,' it said on
a letter Mum got from the hospital. You don't have
to be a medical genius to know that means bad news.
Somehow it didn't make me love Ben any less. It
made me love him more. It made me want to shield
him from anyone who didn't understand, who might
laugh at him, or be embarrassed by him, or look
down on him.

Chapter Three

For the next two years I lived what they call a double life. It sounds romantic when you put it like that, but it was really an awful worry. Home and school were completely separated, or as separated as I could make them. If I ever become an actress, I shall owe my talent to the training of those years. I used to shut the front door every morning playing the part of Dad's Hosanna, and the light of Ben's life, and somewhere between the garden gate and the bus stop, I'd become spotty Anna Peacock (Pee-wit the Pea-brain), the dummy of the second year.

For a long time I didn't mind too much about school. I lived in a dream world, divorced from the realities of everyday life. The awful truth is that I was madly in love with Miss Winter. She had a whiplash body, and short curly hair, and when she slammed the ball over the net in tennis lessons, her shorts sort of flipped up and settled down again on her iron-hard thighs, and I used to feel a dreadful yearning to be saved from a man-eating shark by her. Too embarrassing to remember, really. Having a crush on Miss Winter didn't do me any good, either. I went all numb, and I just let myself in for unnecessary suffering. I still wince at the memory of her shouting at me.

'*Run*, Anna! Where are your arms? For heaven's sake, girl! Hit the ball! Harder! Are you paralysed or something?'

It would have been much more sensible to fall in love with Miss Penny, because English is my best subject, and she liked me as well. But there you are. Love is blind. And it's hard to take a person seriously when their nickname is Spenda. Spenda Penny. Geddit? Anyway, all that kind of thing is far behind me now, I'm thankful to say. I grew out of it months ago.

At home, I was a different person. I belonged to Ben. By the time he was two, he had grown quite big, and his head, of course, was enormous. I knew he wasn't developing in the way that most babies do. I mean, he didn't learn to sit up till he was nearly a year old, and he was only just crawling on his second birthday. I could remember Katy, when she was two, posting shapes into a plastic letter box thing, and stacking up a tower of plastic pots. Mum hadn't even got them out for Ben. I went up to the attic, and fetched them down one day. I didn't see why he shouldn't have normal toys, same as any other kid. Mum looked a bit funny when she saw them.

'Look, Anna,' she said, in the voice of one trying hard to be patient but finding it rather difficult, 'You've got to accept facts. Benny's not like other babies. He's not going to be able to pile up those beakers. He can't even pick things up and hold them properly. And it's no good wishing that he could.'

I was really annoyed with Mum when she said that. Of course I knew Ben was different. What did she take me for? And what did she take Ben for, too? Even if he wasn't normal, he could learn to do some things. He might even get some fun out of it.

'I know, Mum,' I said, in the voice of one trying hard to be polite but finding it rather difficult, 'but I don't see why he can't just look at them, and chew them a bit if he wants to.'

I picked Ben up and he snuggled his great big head down on to my shoulder. He couldn't talk or anything like that, but at long last he'd learned to kiss. I'd spent ages teaching him. You wouldn't believe that learning a little thing like kissing would be so difficult. It took nearly a week getting him to purse his lips, then another week to put them against my cheek, then two to make the actual kiss. One month of solid hard work. But when he did it for the first time, I felt so proud and happy it was like stars exploding inside my head. And Ben went mad with joy. He knew he'd been clever. He laughed and laughed, and beat his weak little arms up and down in the air. Dr Randall had been right about one thing, the night that Ben was born. Laughing was no problem. He could laugh all right.

Mind you, I had second thoughts about teaching Ben to kiss. I began to wish I'd taught him something else. The problem was that once he'd learned how to do it, he wouldn't stop. He never seemed to get bored with it. And no one else, except Mum and sometimes Dad, seemed quite so keen to be kissed by Ben. Even I had to admit that his mouth was wetter than most people's.

'I think it's disgusting,' Katy used to say, looking all prissy, and stuck-up. 'I don't know how you can stand it, getting dribbled all over like that.'

A few weeks earlier, I'd have pinched Katy good and hard for saying that, but I was growing too big for childish squabbles. Anyway, I'd realized that the poor child was suffering from the pangs of jealousy. They were no stranger to me. I knew how it felt to see one's best friend go off with a snotty little sycophant. That was one of my best descriptions of Emma. I'd thought up lots of them, especially last thing at night, but 'snotty sycophant' combined, I thought, strict truthfulness and a neat elegance of phrasing. It was exquisitely crushing. I'd never dared say it to her face, but I was holding it in reserve. One day, I knew, my time for annihilating Emma would come.

I'd realized that Katy was jealous the day she shrieked at me.

'You never play with me like you do with Ben. What have I got to do? Get myself handicapped or something?'

I was just about to tear her limb from limb when I suddenly understood, and a calm feeling of superiority came over me. I felt about fifty years old.

So I smiled at her, and said very kindly, 'Now now, Katy, don't be jealous. Of course I'm really very fond of you.'

But the wretched child just got madder than ever. After that I tried to ignore her. I promised myself that one day I'd do something really stunning for

Katy, like taking her out for a hamburger, or letting her listen to my golden oldie Beatles record. But I kept putting it off. The trouble was, she made me feel guilty. I really did like Ben much better than her. But did that mean I actually preferred him to be handicapped? That would be twisted and selfish. Still, when I thought about it, I decided it was OK. It was best to love Ben just for himself. Wishing couldn't make him any better, but loving him would make him happy. Perhaps that was what Mum had been trying to tell me.

Mum minded much more than I did about him being different. She avoided other babies. She never looked at them, or tickled their tummies in the supermarket like she had done before Ben was born. I suppose she didn't want to think about what he might have been like. She just marched grimly on with him in his pushchair, trying not to see the expressions on people's faces when they caught sight of him.

I didn't mind about the handicap as much as Mum, but I did mind about the way people looked at him. They'd see him, take one long, horrified stare, then their faces would kind of freeze up, and they'd gaze into the distance trying to pretend they hadn't noticed anything. But the minute your back was turned, and you were hunting round the shelves for the cheapest jar of marmalade, you could practically feel their eyes boring into poor, innocent old Ben. He didn't care, mind you. He only went on holding his feet and trying to stuff them into his mouth, just like tiny babies do, only he was two years old.

I used to feel like a gladiator in ancient Rome, girding himself up for battle, before I went to the shops with him. I used to avoid the high street, and walk on a bit further, to the parade furthest away from the school. I'd never met anyone from school there, so I was lulled into a false sense of security. I used to put on his little coat, pull on his mittens, and get ready to stare down anyone who was rude. Actually, I had a worse time than Mum on these expeditions. People didn't dare say anything to her, but just because I looked younger than my age, more like an early thirteen than a middle fourteen, they took all kinds of liberties with me. Once a woman stopped me, and said,

'Do you mind, dear?' and got right down to really stare at Ben, and then said, 'What on earth's the matter with him? I've never seen one as bad as that before.' She gave me a funny look as if she thought I

must be mental or something. I didn't mind children
so much. They used to say what they thought right
out loud, without trying to pretend. Things like,
'Oh look, Mummy. That baby's got such a funny
head.' But I did mind the mothers who would look
round and say '*Shh,*' and pull the kids away. Why
didn't they smile, and say something nice? They
could have said, 'Yes, but he's got lovely curls,'
which was perfectly true. The worst time was when
one horrible old woman with a beard muttered, 'It's
a shame letting a child like that out where a pregnant
woman might see it. Oughtn't to be allowed.'

I was so dumbstruck I couldn't think of a thing to
say. I mean, what would you have done? But luckily
I was in the newsagent's, and Mrs Chapman, who
runs it, is a really nice person. She'd always been
good about Ben.

'Silly old bat,' she said. 'Don't you take any notice
of her, Anna. Ben's lovely, aren't you, my duck?'
and she leaned over her rack of Twixes and Mars
bars so far that her great bosoms got tangled up in
them, and she pulled a funny face at him. Ben went
wild. He always laughed at Mrs Chapman.

I loved her for that. Going to her shop, and seeing
her nice fat body squeeze between the shelves of

sweets and newspapers, and watching her wobble when she bent over Ben to give him a kiss made up for everyone else being funny about us.

'It's kids like this that teach us what loving's all about,' she used to say. 'You mark my words, Anna, they're special. I had a little cousin like this you know. Ray of sunshine, she was.'

In the end, though, it was Mrs Chapman who led to my downfall. I'd gone to the parade on Saturday morning, and was in her shop trying to choose a birthday card for Dad. Men are so difficult to buy things for, I find. One never knows what kind of thing will appeal. Ben was up near the counter, in his pushchair, flapping his hands at Mrs Chapman. I had rejected a joke card with a drunk trying to smoke forty cigarettes at once (it was Dad's fortieth birthday), because I didn't want to encourage him to take up bad habits at his time of life, and I was hesitating over an arty one of a lonely fisherman by a misty lake, when I heard a familiar voice.

'Oh, stop it Greg. Oh, you are awful.'

I froze. It was Miranda. She was the one in my class who was always twined round a boy. She had that kind of tight, bulgy body that seems about to burst out of its clothes, and she knew everything there was to know about sex. I tried not to listen when she got going in the cloakroom. Call me a prig if you like, but I have my standards, and I draw the line at pornography. It degrades women.

My only hope was that Miranda and her horrible Greg would be so wrapped up in each other that they wouldn't notice me, or Ben. But I'd reckoned without Mrs Chapman.

'Here, you two, mind the baby!' she called down the shop, seeing them about to trip over the pushchair. Miranda must have looked at Ben then, because I heard her say, 'Oh my Gawd,' in that silly way she does, and then giggle. I just hoped desperately that they wouldn't see me. I didn't even dare go on looking at the birthday cards. I bent my head right down and looked at the floor. To this day, I could draw you a perfect sketch of the dusty floorboards, complete with all the cracks and knots in the wood. But I didn't get away with it. No such luck.

'Get Ben out of the way, Anna,' Mrs Chapman called to me, really loudly. 'You don't want these love-birds here to do him a mischief.'

There was no help for it then. I had to come out from behind the card stand. I felt my face flush flaming red, and my hands go all wet with sweat. Miranda gasped when she saw me. If I hadn't been so upset I'd have burst out laughing at her. She was so done up she looked ridiculous. I mean, down at the shops on a Saturday morning in our town isn't exactly the same as a Saturday night in Monte Carlo. And green lurex tights on one end of her, and a plunging neckline at the other were too crude for words. But I was too flustered to think up anything witty that would give me the advantage. I wanted to turn tail and run.

'Is this Ben, your brother?' said Miranda, when she'd finally got her bright orange mouth working again.

'Yes it is, actually,' I said, 'and if you've got any questions, comments, sick jokes or wisecracks, now's your chance, Miranda.'

She looked at me then, and I was sorry I'd been so hasty. She didn't look as if she wanted to laugh at all. She just shook her head a bit, and said, 'Knock it off, pea-brain,' in a quiet sort of voice, and trailed out of the shop, towing the deplorable Greg behind her.

I stood there trembling. I didn't know where I was for a moment. The floorboards heaved. Then

I felt Mrs Chapman's enormous soft arm round my shoulder.

'Hey,' she said, 'don't your schoolfriends know about Ben, then?'

I shook my head.

'They didn't,' I said. 'They will now.'

Mrs Chapman gave me a shake.

'Well,' she said, 'you may be a bit upset with me for letting the cat out of the bag, but I'm not going to say I'm sorry. You're a little idiot, Anna. You can't keep something like this a secret. It's high time your schoolfriends knew about it. You're not ashamed of Benny, are you?'

'Course not,' I said, but I knew I was really.

Mrs Chapman did something she'd never done before. She took a Milky Way off the rack, tore off the paper, and gave it to me.

'It's on the house,' she said. 'First, last and only time. Now come on, tell me. Why don't you want your friends to know? What are you so frightened of?'

It isn't easy having a really deep conversation with a newsagent on a Saturday morning. People keep coming in to buy cigarettes, or to ask in husky voices for rude magazines from the top shelves, or to demand sympathy cards suitable for an old person whose goldfish has died. I vowed then and there never to become a shopkeeper. You have to have a butterfly mind. Mine is flighty enough, without giving it any unnecessary encouragement.

Anyway, we managed all right. Mrs Chapman got it all out of me, about how the girls at school didn't like me much, and why I'd kept quiet about Ben because I didn't want to let myself down, and I was afraid of being teased. Then she gave me a good talking to. The funny thing is, I didn't mind. She was so kind, and I knew she was talking sense. I trusted her. It was partly because she'd known and loved a disabled child herself, but it was more than that. Mrs Chapman was wise. She could look into the human heart and plumb its murky depths.

'What are you afraid of, then?' she said. 'Sympathy? Don't be daft, Anna. You can't have too much sympathy in this life. You need it. We all need it. But you've got to learn how to accept it. It's harder to be on the receiving end than the giving end sometimes. And you're not really afraid they'll laugh at you, are you? They're decent kids, deep down. Even that Marina, or Miranda or whatever her name is, she's got a heart, you know. They'll only tease you if you're silly enough to go all proud and prickly, like you did just now, because then you're rejecting them. If you're honest, and open, and say, "Look, it's true, my brother's severely handicapped and I never told you because I felt too miserable about it," I bet you a packet of bacon and onion crisps they'll be very nice about it.

'Why don't you tell them how you're trying to teach Ben things, and show them how much he's learned? He can clap his hands now, can't you, my precious?' and she leaned down, wheezing a bit, and prodded Ben's tummy. He squirmed with pleasure. Then she straightened up again, putting one hand on her back to help herself.

'People are only scared of handicaps because they're not used to them,' she went on. 'You let them get to know Ben, and see how you're so good at looking after him, and I bet they'll be all over him like bees round a honey pot, wanting to love him too.'

Mrs Chapman talked a long time, in between selling pencil sharpeners and tubes of Smarties, but she didn't quite convince me. I could just imagine the sly digs Emma would make, and hear Debbie's cool, unconcerned voice saying rather grandly,

'Well, you fooled us all, didn't you Pee-wit? What made you think we'd be interested anyway?'

But Mrs Chapman was right about one thing. The day after tomorrow I'd have to face them all at school. There was no getting away from that. And being frank and forthright was my only hope. There was no point in being stiff and starchy.

It was an awful long wait until Monday.

Chapter Four

There's a funny thing I've noticed about life. When you really dread something, it turns out to be not so bad. It's the unexpectedly awful things that get you down.

Monday came at last. I'd worked myself up into such a state that Mum finally noticed. Dad hadn't been around much recently. He'd got a new job that kept him late at work, and even away at weekends sometimes. I missed him. I've always got on better with him than with Mum. She's so tactless. I mean, when I got a bit snappy over helping after supper, she ought to have realized I was upset and asked me nicely what the matter was. I was dying to tell her, actually. But instead she just said nastily, 'I don't think I'll bother to cook you a nice supper in future, if you can't be bothered to help clear it up.'

And Katy added her bit by ostentatiously fetching the dishcloth and wiping the table. So naturally, after that, I couldn't say a word.

On the day itself, I got to school early. I decided it would be best to get hold of Debbie on her own, before the whispers had started spreading. Everyone listens to Debbie. If she decided to be nice, I wouldn't have anything to worry about. So I hung round the door into the cloakroom, pretending to read the bit of *David Copperfield* we'd had for homework. That was a big mistake, because old Spenda came past and saw me.

'Do me a favour, Anna, will you?' she said. 'Run over to the staffroom and tell Mr Henry there's a delivery of books waiting for him in the office. Mrs Clark wants them out of her way.'

It was a disaster. There was nothing I could do. I mumbled something that would have been much ruder if I hadn't liked old Spenda so much, and tore off at top speed to get there and back as soon as possible. Just past the gym, I ran into Vicky.

'Do me a favour, will you Vick?' I said. 'Can you take this message to Mr . . .'

'No,' said Vicky, transferring a disgusting blob of gum from one cheek to the other, and looking wide-eyed at me with that maddening grin she puts on when she wants to see how much she can irritate you. No wonder she's a social outcast. I've done my

best for Vicky, like giving her a Christmas card last
year, and sitting beside her at dinner on Thursdays
during Lent, but some people don't want you to be
nice to them.

By the time I'd found Mr Henry and bolted back
to the cloakroom, I'd been ticked off by two teachers
for running in the corridor, and I'd lost my chance
of getting Debbie alone. I could see her smooth
chestnut hair sticking up several inches above a knot
of black, brown and blonde heads, and I could tell
even from a distance that they were all listening,
with riveted attention, to Miranda.

'I've never seen anything like it,' she said. 'I
mean, this great big head, like a monster in a weird
cartoon.'

Something clicked inside me. I dropped my bag
and raced over to the group. They stepped back
when they saw me coming. Every face was agog with
curiosity, and not one displayed even a drop of the
milk of human kindness. Perhaps that was why I was
suddenly possessed by a magnificent anger, held in
check by superhuman force, and the strength of an
iron calm.

'My brother Benedict,' I said to Miranda, 'is not
a monster, and if I ever hear you, or anyone else in

this room, using that word again, I will personally murder you with my bare hands.'

There was a total, unnatural silence. The entire cloakroom, full of about thirty girls, was listening.

'But,' I went on, 'he is severely disabled. He's got hydrocephalus. He'll never be like other children, but he knows how to laugh, and love people, and he's sweet, and adorable, and if you want to know why I didn't tell you before, it's because I knew you'd call him dreadful things, and laugh at him, and he's not a . . . not a . . .' and then I burst into tears.

Looking back, I suppose it was the best thing I could have done, though I felt an awful fool at the time. But I couldn't have kept up the magnificent anger etc for much longer. They all flocked round me, anyway, and I heard Miranda say, 'Honestly, I didn't mean . . .' and Debbie, sounding uncharacteristically furious, saying, 'Shut up, you. You've done enough already.' And then she thrust a tissue into my hand, and said, 'Poor old Pee-wit, you should have told us ages ago. We're really sorry about it. You can see that, can't you?'

And then the bell rang for the first lesson.

The news about Ben spread round the school like wildfire. I knew it would. But I had no idea everyone would be so nice about it.

People kept coming up to me, and saying things like, 'God, how awful,' and 'Poor old Pea-brain,' and offering me bits of chocolate. I usually try not to eat chocolate because of my spots, but I saw each piece as an olive branch, and felt it my duty to accept. Even Emma lent me her pencil sharpener. It was the first time she'd ever been civil. Miranda grabbed me as soon as the bell rang for break.

'Anna, please,' she said. 'I've been feeling so bad. I didn't mean to be horrible. Honestly, I'm really sorry, but you were so . . .'

'I know, I was rude in the shop,' I said. 'It was my fault as much as yours.' I felt magnanimous towards everyone, even Miranda. The truth was that I felt as if a great burden had rolled off my shoulders. I actually bounced when I walked because I felt physically lighter. It was such a relief, such a blissful, wonderful relief to be rid of the secret of Ben, and to find that people seemed to like me more, not less.

On the way to the playground, Mrs Gordon called me into her study. She's the deputy head, and thinks a lot about dignity. I've never felt the same about her since I saw her through a crack in the staffroom door stubbing out a fag, and putting a peppermint into her mouth to take the smell away. It's not that I disapprove of smokers. I know there are people who are victims to a helpless addiction too strong for them to break. But Minnie Gordon had just given us a lecture on health and told us never to touch tobacco. I'm pretty sure she actually denied smoking herself, though I wouldn't swear to it. Old hypocrite. Today, however, she was quite affable, for her.

'Ah, there you are, Anna,' she said. 'I'm sorry to hear about your brother. It must be very hard for your mother.'

There's the typical adult reaction for you. They think that parents are the only ones who are capable of feeling things. They don't realize that it's not exactly easy for brothers and sisters, either.

'You should have told me a long time ago,' she said. 'The school needs to be informed about problems at home.' And she swept past me and on to some pressing duty, pleased with herself for being so grand. But I noticed that her back view was a mess. Her hem was coming down and she'd got a ladder up her tights.

'You've got a problem at home,' I thought. 'Secret drinking, I shouldn't wonder.'

After that, it was just another day – until English in the afternoon. Spenda was making us read poems out loud. They were all about animals. I don't know whether she was being terribly clever or subtle, or whether it was just by accident, but she seemed to choose exactly the right person to read each poem. Debbie did one about an eagle, living 'Close to the sun in azure lands'. Emma read the one about the snake, 'writhing like lightning'. Very appropriate. The next poem was called 'The Donkey'. Spenda looked round the class.

'Your turn, I think, Anna.' She smiled nicely, though.

I like reading poetry aloud. I put in lots of expression and pause dramatically in the right places. Verse one was fine. But as my eye ran on to verse two, the words jumped off the page at me.

With monstrous head and sickening cry
And ears like errant wings . . .

I stood there, dumb as a donkey myself. I couldn't read a word of it.

'Go on, Anna,' said Spenda. 'What's wrong with you?'

'With monstrous head . . .' I began, seeing there was no help for it, and then I caught Debbie's eye. She had her hand over her mouth, and her eyes were dancing, and she was trying desperately not to burst out laughing. Of course, I caught it from her, and started to giggle, and the whole class began to shriek, and we laughed and laughed with poor old Spenda looking round us all, and saying helplessly,

'What on earth's the matter with you all? What's it all about? Will you please stop it, at once!'

That only made us worse, of course. We'd try to stop, but then someone would give a wail of laughter, and we'd all start up again, but eventually she managed to shut us up, and except for the odd gasp and hiccup we got through to the end of the lesson. I'll say one thing for Spenda. She didn't go all huffy and try to make us explain. Goodness knows what we'd have said. She didn't even make us finish reading the poem. She got us going on cruelty to animals instead. It was really interesting.

I felt wonderful after that lesson. The tension had all been laughed away. They'd been laughing with me, not at me. I was one of the crowd again.

*

In games, I plucked up my courage and asked Debbie if she'd like to come home with me after school. I didn't think she'd accept, but she jumped at it. I suspected it was mostly vulgar curiosity, but I didn't blame her. It couldn't hurt Ben, after all. He had no idea what embarrassment was. He'd never been offended in his life.

The surprising thing, though, was Mum's reaction. She looked amazed when she saw Debbie. It's a dreadful thing to admit, but when we came into the kitchen, and I saw her slopping about in her dirty old slippers, with her hair half frizzled and half straight from the perm that was still growing out, I felt ashamed. I saw her through Debbie's eyes, and suddenly realized how much she'd changed over the past two years. I suppose she'd been so tied to the house with Ben and everything that she'd stopped bothering about herself. It had been ages since she'd bought herself something new, or even put on any make-up.

'Where's Ben?' I said.

I saw her eyes open with alarm.

'He's asleep,' she said. 'You can't . . .' but at that moment I heard him crowing. There must have been a pigeon on his windowsill because that always made him laugh. I put bread out specially to attract them. If one was pecking away when Ben woke up, he'd open his eyes and start laughing right off. It was the happiest noise you could imagine.

I couldn't wait to get Debbie out of the kitchen, before she could notice the stains on Mum's apron, or the hole in her tights. I pushed her out of the door, and off up the stairs, my heart hammering.

Ben was in his cot. He had learned to sit up by himself, and I was trying to teach him to reach up for the top rail and pull himself up to a standing position. He hadn't got there yet, but we were working on it. When he saw me, he did what he always did, reached out his arms and roared with joy. I lifted him up, and danced round the room with him. I was putting off the moment when I'd have to look at Debbie.

When I did, I couldn't see her face. She was bending over her bag, and then she straightened up with a chocolate bar in her hand.

'Is he allowed to eat it?' she said.

'Oh he loves chockies, yummy yummy chockies, don't you my little Benny-Ben?' I said. I knew I sounded silly, but I couldn't stop prattling. I was too nervous. But then I shot a look at Debbie, and shut up. She was gazing at Ben with a really concentrated expression. It wasn't nasty prying, it was interested, even kindly.

'Does it hurt?' she said. 'His head must be difficult to hold up, it's so big and such a funny shape.'

'No, it doesn't seem to hurt,' I said. I'd sort of calmed down because she was being so matter-of-fact. 'It's awful when he gets a cold though. He really has to fight for breath. Mum's been up with him all through the night ever so often.'

'She must be shattered,' said Debbie. 'I'm a wreck if I don't get my eight hours. I don't know how she does it.'

'She's got to do it. She doesn't have much choice,' I said. Actually, I hadn't really thought about it before. Mum had been getting up in the night for so long that I'd got used to it. I'd stopped asking myself how she managed. I just took it for granted.

Debbie's mind is so transparent that you can practically see the cogs going round. That's the good thing about her. She's incapable of being deceitful. She can be infuriating, and mean, and cutting, and fickle but you'll always know where you are with her. She's sort of detached from life, as if she was peering at other mortals down a microscope, or from outer space or something. It gets her into awful trouble. I'll never forget the time Mrs Gordon lost her temper because Debbie had let a door swing shut in Mrs G's face, and Debbie said 'Sorry,' in such a cool, unconcerned voice that Mrs G went raging mad. Debbie just stood there watching her with a kind of scientific interest. When Mrs G stopped to draw breath, and stick a few hairpins back into her scraggy grey chignon, Debbie said, as cool as a cucumber, 'Excuse my saying so, Mrs Gordon, but I think you ought to see the dentist. You've got bad breath.'

Mrs Gordon stood there for a moment, as one turned to stone, then shut her mouth with a snap and marched off to report Debbie to the head, but nothing ever came of it. Emma said the head probably fainted at the stench of Mrs G's breath, and told her she was an undesirable alien. The funny thing was, though, that Debbie was really surprised about all the fuss. She said she'd only been giving Mrs G some well-meant advice, and she should have been grateful.

So I wasn't surprised when Debbie asked a lot of impertinent questions about Ben. I didn't mind a bit. Then I said, 'Would you like to hold him?'

Her scientific detachment deserted her all of a

sudden, and she looked a bit nervous, blinking those big, beautiful brown eyes of hers, and shaking her sleek brown hair out of them. She stepped back.

'I might hurt him, or drop him or something,' she said. 'I don't know about babies.'

'Don't be a fool,' I said, and plopped him straight into her arms.

She held him stiffly for a minute, then tried to turn him round. Once she'd done it, and Ben was directly opposite her face, the result was inevitable. He pushed out his lips, and kissed her cheek. Unfortunately, I'd already given him a piece of chocolate bar, and some sticky brown dribble was running down his chin.

Debbie is one of the most fastidious people I know. She gets up at dawn every day to wash her hair, and she told me when she stopped being my best friend that though she liked my personality, she couldn't face my spots, buck teeth and greasy hair. They offended her aesthetic sensibilities. It hurt terribly at the time, but I know she didn't mean to be unkind. It was just the sort of horribly frank and honest thing that Debbie was always saying. She thought she was giving me a perfectly reasonable explanation.

I stood waiting for her to look disgusted and thrust

Ben back at me. But instead she looked startled.

'He kissed me!' she said. 'Or was it an accident?'

'No, I taught him to kiss,' I said. 'It took ages. I'd no idea there was so much skill in it.'

'But that's amazing,' said Debbie, wiping her cheek. 'I thought he'd be a kind of living lump, just eating, and breathing. Do you mean he can actually learn things, and make friends with people, like an ordinary person?'

If anyone else had said that, I'd have thumped them. Living lump indeed! But you have to keep reminding yourself that Debbie's a special case. She's socially primitive. She only gets away with it because she's so beautiful.

'Of course he can learn things,' I said. 'I've taught him to clap his hands. Watch this.'

She put Ben down on the floor, and he performed perfectly.

'What else can he do?' said Debbie.

'I'm trying to teach him to stand up,' I said. 'Look.'

I pushed my fingers into Ben's closed fists. He grasped them, and I pulled him up on to his feet. He stood there for a moment, frowning earnestly, then plumped down on to his bottom again, and laughed.

You could see he was pleased with himself.

Debbie was quite enthusiastic.

'You could teach him all sorts of things,' she said. 'He might even catch up if you worked hard enough. You could teach him to talk.' She picked up Ben's hand and pointed at it.

'Hand,' she said, very loudly, 'Say "hand".'

'You can't do that,' I said. 'It'll be years before he learns to say anything. And he might not, even then. There's no point in ever thinking he'll be the same as other kids. He just won't. You've got to be realistic, and start from where he's at. Even learning the simplest things, like putting a chocolate bar in his mouth, are like climbing Mount Everest to him.'

Ben had curled his fingers round one of Debbie's, and was staring at it. You could see he was concentrating hard. Debbie must have liked the feel of it, because she said,

'I think he's cute. Sort of different and special. I wish you'd told me about him before, Anna. I'd like to have seen him when he was tiny. It must be fun, teaching him things. Can I come back and see him again?'

'Yes,' I said, 'oh yes, any time you like, Debbie, any time at all.'

She picked up her bag and slung it over her shoulder with the kind of easy grace I'll never learn even if I live to a hundred and three and do yoga exercises every day.

'Goodbye then,' she said. 'See you tomorrow.'

'I thought you'd stay for tea,' I said, trying not to look disappointed.

'Can't,' she said, 'I've got choir practice tonight.'

I went downstairs with her, and saw her out. Then I shut the front door, and turned to see Mum behind me. She'd changed, and done her hair, and put some make-up on.

'I thought Debbie was staying for tea,' she said.

'No, she's got choir tonight,' I said.

Mum looked uncertain. I knew what she wanted to ask, and I knew she wouldn't be able to.

'I told them at school about Ben today,' I said, putting her out of her misery. 'Miranda saw me last week with him, and it was all round the class. I thought they'd be awful, but they were really nice. I wish I'd told everyone years ago. And Mum, Debbie likes him. She really does. She thinks he's special, and she'd like to come again.'

I didn't wait for that sort of remote look that comes over Mum's face whenever I mention Debbie.

She thinks Debbie's a little Madam, and gets away with murder, and needs her bottom spanking. Mum doesn't understand that beauty and charm exact their toll. I was so pleased that I ran down the hall, and took a running jump at the light. I used to do that a lot when I was a kid, but it's not the sort of thing you do much when you're fourteen. I hadn't reckoned on the fact that I'd grown, so instead of just tipping the shade a bit with my fingers, I gave it a proper whack by mistake, and it swung about wildly. I thought Mum would be irritated, but she laughed.

'You look happy today,' she said. 'It was lovely to see you coming in with a friend, like you used to. It's been a long time.'

'Yes,' I said, 'and it's lovely seeing you look so nice and pretty, with lipstick and everything. That's been a long time too.'

'I didn't want to let you down in front of Debbie,' she said. 'Give me a bit more warning next time.'

We stood there, like a pair of idiots, smiling at each other. Then Mum said,

'Come on, let's have a cup of tea,' and I said, 'Why not?' and we settled down at the kitchen table like a couple of real grown-up friends having a chat.

I'd never felt sort of equal with Mum before, like I was a woman, and understood her problems, but I did that afternoon. We didn't say much, just little things, like how Ben was getting on learning to stand, and how awful it was Dad never being around at weekends, and I said why didn't Mum leave Ben with me on Saturday and go down to the shops, and buy herself something nice to wear, and Mum said why didn't she make me an appointment at the new salon in the high street to have my hair cut, and then she suddenly looked at the clock, and said,

'Oh Lord, I've got to pick Katy up from Tracey's party.'

I laughed, and said, 'Bet she insisted on wearing her party shoes to school today,' and Mum laughed too and said, 'You know what she's like.' Then she went, and I did the washing-up without her asking me, and set the table for supper, and settled Ben down in front of the TV because there was a pop music show on, and he loved listening to music. And I felt about twenty-five years old, and mature, and grown up, and wise.

Chapter Five

The summer that Ben was two is bathed in a rosy sort of sunset in my memory. I can't believe I was so carelessly happy, or that I didn't have a premonition of what was going to happen. It was one of those long, hot summers, when the days seem to go on for ever, and everyone is lazy and languorous, and people stop bothering to make you tidy your room, and it's fatally easy to fall in love.

It didn't start off well, though. We were all depressed because we couldn't go away for a holiday. Katy pestered Mum and Dad on and on for a week on the Costa del Sol. Her friend Tracey had gone there, so Katy thought it was the last word in cosmopolitan sophistication. I wouldn't have minded a holiday there myself, I must say, but I knew better than to nag. I finally dragged Katy off into my bedroom and gave her a proper talking to.

'Will you shut up about holidays?' I said. 'Can you imagine us on an aeroplane, with Ben? How do you think it would feel pushing him up and down the promenade in Benidorm? Do you fancy feeding him his breakfast in a crowded hotel dining room?'

Comprehension dawned. I'll say one thing for Katy, she's not slow. Then she scowled, and kicked my bed. She did it harder than she meant to, and hurt her toe, and had to hop round the room holding on to her foot.

'Ben!' she said, when she was finally capable of saying anything. 'It's always Ben! Mum won't take me swimming because she can't leave Ben. I couldn't have a proper birthday like Tracey's because Mum's so tired looking after Ben. Now we can't even go on holiday like a proper, ordinary family. I sometimes wish . . .'

'What do you sometimes wish, Miss?' I said, my voice dangerously quiet and menacing. Katy knew I'd scalp her if she wasn't careful, so she just said sulkily, 'Oh nothing.'

'I suppose you think we should put Ben in some horrid home, with cruel nurses, while we go off and have a good time?' I said, with awful sarcasm. She pouted.

'I suppose you wouldn't care if he got one of his colds, and there was no one there he knew to pick him up in the night and comfort him,' I went on, remorselessly.

Katy suddenly jumped up and turned on me.

'Of course I would,' she said. 'Don't be such a pig! I don't want him to be miserable.' And she darted out of my room, and I heard her crashing down the stairs and out into the garden, where Ben was sitting as good as gold in his playpen, studying a leaf that had fallen into it. And she danced round him singing,

'We all live in a yellow submarine,' in her high-pitched, tuneless voice while Ben clapped his hands and shrieked as he always did. That's another good thing about Katy, I must admit. Underneath her irritating exterior she's got a kind little heart. She'll stick by you if you're really in trouble. It's just that you have to be really in trouble first.

Mind you, I'm not saying that I didn't care about the holiday. Of course I did. When I was little, we used to rent a cottage in the country, for two weeks in August, a different one every year. There was no thrill like the excitement of following the written instructions, and arriving, and piling out of the car, and exploring the whole place, and deciding who would sleep in which bedroom. Each cottage had something specially nice about it. One, I remember, had an old apple tree in the back garden that you could climb. I spent whole afternoons up there, with a cushion, an apple, and a book. Another had a field beside it with ponies in it, and I used to go and feed them handfuls of grass every morning, and whisper things into their soft, flickering ears, that smelled deliciously of horse. But there was no point in wishing. I knew quite well that we had to stay at home.

Dad knew it was tough for us, seeing our friends go away. I overheard him and Mum talking about it one night. I didn't mean to snoop, but they were in the garden, and I was in my bedroom, with the window open, and it was one of those still summer nights when sound carries further than usual.

'Katy was very grumpy at bedtime tonight,' said Mum. 'I can't think what gets into that child sometimes.'

'She had a postcard from Tracey this morning, from Spain,' said Dad. 'Poor old thing's feeling left out.'

That was typical of Mum and Dad. She couldn't work out what the matter was, but Dad seemed to just know. There was a silence, then Mum gave a big sigh.

'I suppose we couldn't, could we?' she said, a little uncertainly. 'Of course we couldn't,' said Dad, in his crisp, I-am-the-manager-of-this-firm voice. 'And if anyone needs a holiday, it's you. The girls will just have to take second place at the moment. Look, we could get a nurse in for a few nights, and I'd manage in the day. I could take a week off. They owe me that at least after all I've been doing for the last six months. And you could go off for a week with Janice, or your mother.'

'No!' said Mum, and her voice sounded sort of cracked. 'I couldn't leave him! Every time it gets worse. Oh, Peter, if only you'd been here when he had that cold last month. It was no more than a chill, and honestly he was fighting for his life. I don't know how I'll bear it . . .' and then I heard her crying, and Dad moving his chair, and then muffled noises, so I shut the window, because although I couldn't help listening to them talking, I didn't want to hear them kissing and everything. It turns me off when old people do it.

They must have talked some more, because the next morning, at breakfast, Dad still had on his bright, breezy, organizing manner that he gets sometimes, when he decides that things have got too slack at home and it needs a man to put them right. He'd been up to the shops before breakfast, and had come back with croissants and the local paper. He took Mum's breakfast up to her on a tray. Ben had been awake a lot in the night, he said, and she needed to sleep in. Then he unfolded the paper and made a great show of finding the 'Summer events for children' column.

'Ah!' he said at last, and pushed his glasses down to the tip of his nose so he could pretend to look intellectual.

'Swimming. Daily courses in life-saving and diving. Ages five to eleven.'

'It's booked up, Daddy. Mum phoned last week,' Katy said. She was in a mood, and would have turned down tea at Buckingham Palace if she'd been invited.

'Riding,' Dad read out. Katy's eyes brightened. She looked interested in spite of herself. Dad looked down the advert and saw the prices.

'On second thoughts, bad idea,' he said. 'Riding develops the bottom. Turns to fat in middle age,' and went on hastily to the next item.

'Outward bound.'

I gave him a look.

'Dad . . .' I said. He looked up at me, and smiled.

'OK, OK,' he said. 'Say no more.'

An advert on the opposite page caught his eye.

'Wedding dress, size twelve, unused, only twenty-five pounds. Mmm, they must have quarrelled at the last minute. I wonder if they're trying to sell the cake as well?'

I could see his mind had wandered and it would take a week to get it back on course again, so I tweaked the paper out of his hand.

'Here, do you mind?' he said. But I had found what I was looking for.

'Tennis course, two hours daily, professional coaches, places still available.'

'There you are,' I said triumphantly. 'That's what I want to do.'

I didn't dare tell anyone, but I'd been nursing a secret ambition. It was partly because I'd been watching Wimbledon all through June, but it was also the result of a freak streak of brilliance I'd suddenly developed in the last week of the summer term. I had astonished myself by a series of ace serves, and a spate of shots which made even Debbie gasp. In the very last lesson before the holidays, I was playing doubles with Miranda against Miss Winter and Sandra. I suddenly astounded everyone by foreseeing the exact angle at which Miss Winter's wicked top spin whizzed over the net, and ricocheted off the tarmac, and then positioning myself exactly right and whacking it back with such precision that it skimmed the net and flew between Sandra's legs before she had time to jump. So sweet had been the praises that had fallen from everyone's lips (I had grown out of my hopeless passion for Miss Winter but retained a kind of loyalty to the sacred memory of love), and so delightful the shoulder clappings I received as I modestly retired from the court, that I had decided to work my game up into something really sensational, and spring it on an astonished world next summer.

Dad was delighted. He had solved the problem of how I would spend my time. Now he only had to deal with Katy. I could see he was already congratulating himself on being so well organized and resourceful.

He had underestimated Katy. Half an hour later, she had driven us both to screaming point. She had turned down a drama workshop, ballet lessons, a sports week, trampolining and junior watersports. She had refused to go and stay with Granny, Aunty Janice and the Watsons, who used to be our next-door neighbours, but moved a year ago. She had insisted that, since she couldn't go to Benidorm like Tracey, she would spend every day at home, sulking, and too bad if we didn't like it. She had entirely forgotten our little talk of the day before. That's the trouble with children. They can't stick to anything. Once they get an idea in their heads they bring it up again and again, and there's no point your thinking that you've knocked it out, because you haven't.

'All right,' said Dad at last. 'I give up. It's tennis lessons for one, sulks for the other. Katy can make herself useful at home minding Ben.'

Katy could not stop herself looking anxious.

'I'll go and telephone the tennis place now,' said Dad, 'and fix it all up for you, Spanner.' He spent a long time putting the newspaper together again. I could see he was giving Katy a last chance to change her mind. She fell for it.

'Well, I suppose, if I've got to, I could do tennis too,' she said at last. I sighed. Typical. She would want to do the same as me. Now I'd have her trailing after me every day, cramping my style, nosing into everyone I spoke to and being a general nuisance. I was so irritated I slammed the door as I went out, not quite loud enough to get ticked off for, but enough to make my feelings plain to everyone sensitive enough to read the signs. I knew it would do no good to protest. I was stuck with Katy, and I might as well accept it.

Actually, when I'd calmed down, it didn't seem such a bad idea. I realized that she could be quite useful. It probably wouldn't be easy to get enough people to practise with. If Katy only learned to get the ball over the net, I could practise smashing them back. And she'd never complain. It would be better than nobody, anyway. Not much better, but still better. I decided to go downstairs quickly again, and pretend that it had been the wind that had slammed the door, and see if Dad would give me some money for new trainers and a racket. He might even be so relieved and pleased with himself for sorting out our summer holidays that he'd pay for one of those pretty tennis outfits like the stars at Wimbledon wear. It was worth a try, anyway.

So that was how it all began, that happy, carefree summer, the last of my untrammelled youth.

If I'm going to be absolutely honest, I must admit that it wasn't only the tennis that was luring me down to the courts. It was Ted's Snackbar too. The tennis courts were in a corner of the Recreation Ground, which was just a field, with some trees round the edge, and a playground with things like swings and sandpits. Between the swings and the courts was this kind of open air café. It was only a hut really, where old Ted sold coffee and tea, and ices, but you could watch any games going on on the courts, and mess about on the swings, if the parkkeeper wasn't there (they were supposed to be out of bounds for the over fourteens). Old Ted didn't take any notice of what anyone did. He just read his newspaper all day, and only popped his head out when there was somebody waiting to put some money into his grubby old till. Anyway, that was where the scene was that summer. Miranda had practically lived there since the end of term. She was always shrieking around, and showing off, and then disappearing behind a tree with one of the boys.

I didn't want to be like Miranda, exactly, but I did want to see what was going on. I wanted to sort of try myself out a bit. Since that day when Debbie had come home with me, my life had really changed. Mum had started to notice me for the first time for years. She seemed to realize that I was now more than ten years old. She'd even had a blitz on my looks. She'd got me contact lenses, and made me go to an expensive hairdresser who had given me a different sort of shampoo so my hair wasn't quite so greasy. I still had spots, but they were getting better, only a couple at a time, and sometimes none at all. Dare I say it, I looked quite good sometimes. Even Debbie noticed a change in me.

'It's not that you're pretty, exactly,' she said, wrinkling up her perfect nose while I waited anxiously for the verdict, 'though you've got a touch of style now, I must say. It's more . . . it's like there's a kind of electricity in you that gives off a flash from time to time, and then you kind of radiate. It's cool.'

Emma hated it when Debbie took any notice of me, and she'd put her word in at once.

'We'd better keep out of your way then,' she said, giggling in that awful moronic way of hers, 'or we'll get contaminated with the fall-out when you have one of your c-o-o-l flashes.'

Debbie hadn't laughed, but she hadn't stopped Emma from dragging her away either. I think she was too lazy to resist Emma's iron will.

Nothing much happened the first few afternoons down at the Rec. There weren't many people about, and Miranda didn't come at all. But on Thursday afternoon, the place was suddenly crowded. As luck would have it, I was looking really good. Dad had been generous about the tennis stuff. I had these great trainers, and a really nice dress. I'd pointed out to him that he was saving himself a fortune by not taking us all to the Costa del Sol, and he'd taken the hint. I was wearing my lenses too. I'd got to the point where I could keep them in for about four hours without wanting to scratch my eyes out.

At the end of every lesson, Terry (the coach) and I used to play a few proper games, and I was in the middle of my serve when I saw Miranda and the gang coming. I did a double take. I was suddenly terrified in case any underarm hair was popping out of my short sleeve when I lifted up my arm, so I twisted myself round to serve, so that they'd only see the back of my shoulder, and nearly ruptured myself bringing the racket down on the ball at a funny angle. There was a sort of grunt, and a squeak of amazement from Terry, because by some incredible chance it had turned into a smashing ace, and he'd had to duck to avoid being assassinated.

'Brilliant, Anna!' he boomed, scratching his hairy chest in the gap where his button-up T-shirt was gaping open. Terry had some revolting personal habits, but he was a fantastic coach. He made good tennis come as easily as eating bread and honey.

I saw Miranda's head swivel round when she heard my name, and I could see her sort of squinting at me against the sun, through her great mop of hair, trying to decide if it was me or not. Then Katy, who was kicking herself round on one of those playground carousel things while she was waiting for me to finish with Terry, called out, 'Hello, Miranda!' and Miranda recognized her and realized it must be me.

Miranda may be boy-mad, but she's not one of the sort who won't have anything to do with other girls. She's got a friendly nature. That's her problem, Mum always says. Too friendly by half. Anyway, she shook off the boy who'd got his arm draped round her neck, and came to shout encouragement at me through the wire netting. I saw she was carrying a racket.

'You going to play, then?' I said.

'Yeah,' she said. 'We're doing doubles.'

'Who's "we"?' I asked.

'Oh, me and Joe against Barny and Tony.'

I didn't have time for any more, because Terry was working on my backhand, and he kept shoving one awful ball at me after the other, but I saw them out of the corner of my eye as they went into the next court. I knew Joe and Barny vaguely. I'd seen them at the youth club I used to go to ages ago. I didn't recognize the other one. But funnily enough, even though I only saw him out of the corner of my eye, I was aware of him at once. He had that kind of pantherish walk, sort of elegant, but full of suppressed power that you felt might break out at any minute.

Then Terry and I changed ends, because the sun was right in his eyes, and he said at my age I could stand it better than him, so I walked round the net on the side nearest Miranda's court, and got a closer look.

I've noticed something really interesting about first impressions. When I see someone for the first time, before I've even talked to them or anything, I get a kind of instant glimpse of what they're really like. Then, when I get to know them a bit, the picture changes and they seem quite different. But once I get to know them really well, I often find that the very first impression was nearer the truth than the second one.

That's how it was with Tony. I can see him now as I first saw him, just as if I had a photograph of him in my head. He was standing a bit apart from the

other three, and listening to them, not smiling, but
looking rather remote. His dark hair fell in a heavy
shock over his forehead, and his eyes were brilliant
and direct, with long dark lashes that made them
look even bigger. His mouth had a kind of twist to it,
that could have been mocking, or unhappy. I could
see that Miranda was smitten. She kept wriggling out
of Joe's reach, though she'd been happily making a
spectacle of herself with him all over town since the
end of last term, and edging up towards Tony. He
kept moving away, not nastily, but in an almost too
polite kind of way that made him seem dignified
and untouchable, and above all that kind of thing.
But I could see, in that first, brilliant snapshot, that
he wasn't at all cold and withdrawn in the way he
seemed. I could sense someone else in him, someone
intense, and lonely, and locked up. It sounds corny,
I know, but so what? The corniest things are usually
the truest, I think anyway.

Their game started. Mine was nearly over. They
weren't very good, at least, Tony wasn't bad. He
had a natural kind of speed and grace, but he didn't
seem to have played tennis much. Once, while he
was waiting for Barny to take Joe's serve, I saw that
he was watching me, and I'd just done a particularly

showy save from the net. Then Terry started one of his firework volleys that sent the ball over again and again as fast as a meteor shower. When I finally missed the last one, it crashed into the wire netting that separated the two courts, and I crashed after it, because I'd been running so fast to get it, and as luck would have it, at exactly the same moment, Tony was retrieving a ball from the same spot on the other side. We were suddenly only a couple of inches away from each other. I think I must have given off one of my electric flashes, because I saw a tiny answering spark in his brown eyes, then he dropped his eyelids and said 'Sorry'. I can't think why, because we hadn't actually bumped into each other or anything, and then he strolled back to his game.

That was all it was, that first meeting. But it was enough to pierce my lousy defences, which, when it came to love, were absolutely useless. And I kept telling myself I was being an outsize, number one, prize-winning twit. Tony was by far the most attractive boy I'd ever seen. And with all the Mirandas of this world trailing after him, I would never have a look-in.

Usually, after I'd finished with Terry, Katy and I had an ice cream at Ted's, and then we went

home, but that day I was desperate to stick around.
I pretended to be listening to Terry's little lecture,
the one he always gives at the end of a coaching
session, when all the time I was trying to think of
a good excuse for not going home. In the end, I
needn't have bothered. Good old Katy came to my
rescue. She walked up to the netting, bold as brass,
and called out, 'Miranda! Hey, Miranda! Do you
want me to ball-boy?'

Of course, Miranda said yes. Then as an
afterthought, Katy said, 'You don't mind, do you,
Annie?' and I said, as casually as I could, 'No, that's
OK,' and then I got a Coke from Ted, and sat down
on the swing, with my right side facing the courts
because my hair's parted on the left so my right
profile is the best one.

I must have sat there for half an hour at least.
Usually, I can't bear just sitting around with nothing
to do. I can't even bear to go to the loo if I haven't
got something to read in there. In fact, I've had
several near misses hunting for a book to take in with
me. Mad, really. But that day I could have sat there
for ever.

It was partly the sun, filtering through the trees,
and making the boring old Rec look mellow and

dignified, like a park round a stately home (except that the back end of the Colliston Road flats couldn't possibly be mistaken for a stately home), and partly the hypnotic effect of the swing, which had a rhythmic sort of sing-song squeak, and lifted my hair in a lovely warm breeze every time I went forward. But of course, it was mainly being near Tony, and wondering what would happen when the game was over.

My lovely daydream of being a kind of countess or something, and having tea under the big elm on the south lawn from a tray that the butler had set up on a white Italian style table, was rudely shattered when Katy suddenly yelled 'Mum!' and dashed out of the court, and raced off over the grass where Mum had appeared, pushing Ben in the pushchair.

I stopped swinging then. I hadn't bargained for Ben that afternoon. Barny and Joe were all right. I didn't care about them. And Miranda had seen Ben lots of times. I'd even taken him to school one day. Spenda had got us to do a project on disabled people, and Ben had come along to meet the class. He'd been a wow. In fact, dear old Ben had become a kind of mascot. The numbers of useless jackets the girls had knitted for him, you wouldn't believe. But it was Tony I was wondering about. I couldn't guess what his reaction would be.

They finished their game, and came out of the court just as Mum arrived at the swings. Ben was wriggling about fretfully.

'He saw a little girl over there with an ice cream,' said Mum. 'Can you get him one, Anna?'

She gave me some money, and I went over to Ted's. By the time he'd put his paper down, and fished around in his freezer, and dug out Ben's favourite lolly, poor old Ben was crying properly. I peeled the paper off and gave it to him, then looked around for Tony. He'd gone. All I could see was his back, as he ran lightly down the path, on to the main road, towards the bus stop.

Chapter Six

It was odd going back to school after the summer. They'd switched all the classes round. I'd been with Debbie, and Sandra, and Vicky and Miranda and all the rest of them ever since I was eleven, and all of a sudden there were a lot of different faces. I felt quite lost for a week or two. I mean, if you've spent half your waking life with the same bunch of people for years and years you get sort of dependent on them whether you really like them or not, and when half of them aren't there any more, you feel strange. It's like moving house or something.

Debbie and Emma were still in my class, and so was Miranda. They were doing arts subjects like me. But Vicky and Gloria, as well as Sandra and all her clever friends, had gone into the science class. I'd never got on with them much. They were too high-powered. But they were better than the load of silly gigglers we got instead. Karen and Bella were the worst. I couldn't help despising them. I know you shouldn't be an intellectual snob, but they seemed to have got stuck at the mental age of nine. They were awful in English lessons. They couldn't take literature seriously. I'd got quite keen on it, actually. I used to read Keats in bed, and learn chunks off by heart. I thought it was so awful the way he died so young, and everything. I tried writing some poems myself sometimes, and left them on my desk, hoping that Mum would read them and tell me they were brilliant. But she just tidied everything into a heap when she did my room, and never seemed to notice. Just like her.

We had a new English teacher, Mrs Hamilton. She'd got white hair, but she had it cut fashionably, as if she was still only eighteen or something. It looked clever and sort of timeless. I wished my mum would be a bit less boring about her clothes and everything. When I'm forty I'm going to stay in tune with youth. I'm going to remember exactly what it's like to be fifteen, and I'm going to have deep and special sympathy with unattractive girls. And that's a promise.

Mrs Hamilton wasn't just interesting to look at. She did odd things too. She used to stride up and down, throwing out her hands in striking gestures so that her gold bangles clunked together. But the minute there was anything the slightest bit sexy, Karen would start sniggering and set Bella off.

Mrs Hamilton bore it for a week or two, and then she struck. We were doing poets of the seventeenth century, and she was reading Andrew Marvell.

An hundred years should go to praise
Thine eyes and on the forehead gaze.

Clunk went her bracelets. Karen opened her eyes wide, and gazed on Bella's forehead, and Bella dropped her head on to her desk while her shoulders started heaving. Mrs Hamilton had marched up to the back of the class as she was reading, and her long, full skirt swished round as she turned.

Two hundred to adore each breast

– the words rang out richly, but at the word 'breast' Bella cracked right out laughing. Mrs Hamilton must have been expecting it, because she was right behind Bella's chair.

'Stand *up*!' she said, barking out '*Up*' so loudly and suddenly that Bella was startled out of her giggles.

'Hold your head up, Bella,' said Mrs Hamilton. 'I want everyone to see you. Now then, how old are you?'

'Fifteen,' said Bella, beginning to look sulky.

'Fancy,' said Mrs Hamilton. 'I thought perhaps you were thirteen and had got into this class by mistake.'

She was terrific at sarcasm. I bet she'd wanted to go on the stage, and her parents had said, 'It's so uncertain dear, better take a teaching diploma.' Awful waste of talent if you ask me. Bella was beginning to go pink.

'And have you had the facts of life explained to you?' said Mrs Hamilton. Her voice was all silky now. Sort of sweet, and treacherous, and sadistic if you know what I mean.

'Yes, Mrs Hamilton,' said Bella.

'Oh?' said Mrs Hamilton. 'I thought perhaps you had culled all your information from the gutter press or the playground. I must have a word with whoever it is who does sex education with your class. Who is it, Bella?'

Bella mumbled.

'You've finished sex education? Perhaps I should arrange a refresher course in sex education for you.' She was looking round the class as she spoke, obviously hoping we were admiring her performance, and joining in with her against Bella. I thought that was going over the top. It's one thing getting the better of someone who's being silly, but I don't see why she had to drag the rest of us into it. Everyone was feeling uneasy now, and shuffling, and looking down. Mrs Hamilton sensed it. See what I mean about being the great actress who never was? She knew exactly how to play her audience. She knew how much we could take, and when she'd gone too far she back-pedalled. She stopped looking round and her voice lost its heaviness and just became lightly ironic.

'I think perhaps, Bella,' she said, 'that in future we'll warn you if there's anything too mature in our poetry lessons, and you can go and join the second years for a while. Mm?'

Bella said nothing. Her face was puce, and she was squirming inside.

'But on second thoughts, perhaps you'd like to have another chance of showing that you can cope with adult matters,' said Mrs Hamilton, and her voice had suddenly gone back to normality, nice and brisk and ordinary. It took the sting out of what she'd been saying.

'You can sit down now, you silly girl, and don't let it happen again.'

And of course, it never did. After a week or two the effect wore off a bit, and Karen started nudging people when there was anything the slightest bit 'rude', but Mrs Hamilton only had to pause for a moment, and put her head on one side in a questioning kind of way, and give her one look, and Bella's knowing smile froze on her lips, and her giggle sort of died in her throat. By half-term, Mrs Hamilton could declaim anything she liked, and we were all carried away by it.

I would have thought that Miranda would have been one of the worst of the gigglers, but she wasn't. She'd changed since the summer holidays. She was much nicer. In fact, we'd got to be really good friends. Her parents had split up a few months earlier. Her mother had gone off to live with someone else, and she and her Dad had moved. They lived quite near us now. Miranda didn't talk about her parents much. She just said it had got easier, because before her parents had always had such awful rows, especially at night, and their flat had been very small, and she'd heard every word, and her mother had never liked her much anyway. So now, at last, there was some peace and quiet.

I couldn't imagine what it would be like. I mean, I'd never imagined Mum and Dad splitting up or anything. They'd had rows, of course. In fact, they'd got worse recently. I could remember that a long time ago they'd seemed happier, before Mum got so tired with Ben, and when Dad wasn't going away so much. But I'd never thought anything could go seriously wrong.

Miranda and I went home together most days now. There was often a wait for the bus, then quite a long walk at the end, so we had plenty of time to talk. I was horribly fascinated by her awful family. I could hardly believe some of the things she told me. But she seemed just as interested in mine.

'Hasn't your mum ever tried to put Ben into a home?' she asked one day, as we walked up the hill, past the shops, lugging our great big bags full of the homework that Mrs Hamilton had piled on to us.

'Of course not,' I said scornfully. 'She was upset when he was born, but she adores him now. Who wouldn't? I mean, you wouldn't put him in a home if he was yours, would you?'

Miranda had become one of Ben's biggest fans.

She wasn't like Debbie, who took an intellectual interest in seeing how much he could learn. She just liked cuddling him, and calling him silly names, and talking baby talk. A normal two-year-old would have got bored and fed up probably, but Ben could go on being tickled and cuddled and cooed over for ever.

'My mum wouldn't even have brought him back from the hospital,' said Miranda.

'Of course she would,' I said, not really listening. I'd seen a boy in the distance, walking away from us, who looked a bit like Tony, and I watched hard till he turned down a side road. But then I saw his face and realized it was someone else. That happened about a hundred times a week, and I still hadn't got used to it.

'No, honestly,' Miranda was saying. 'She never wanted to have kids. Would you believe it, she even tried to have an abortion when she was expecting me? But it didn't work.'

'What?' That stopped me dead in my tracks. I was listening hard enough now. 'How do you know?'

'She told me one day when she was in a specially evil temper. She was sorry afterwards, and said it wasn't true, but I know it was. I could *feel* it was.'

Miranda shrugged as if she didn't care, but I could

see the most awful pain in her face.

'My God,' I said. I mean, what do you say when someone tells you a thing like that? That her own mother tried to get rid of her before she was born? 'But she must have loved you and everything, once she actually saw you,' I went on, feebly.

'Not really,' said Miranda. 'She did her duty by me, I suppose, but never anything extra. Not like your mum. She really likes you. You can tell. Anyway –' she suddenly wanted to change the subject. 'I don't care any more. I'm grown up now. I don't need parents. I can look after myself. I'm going to be quite different from her. I'm going to have lots of babies, and I'm going to love them all.'

'Yes,' I said, 'but mind you don't go and have one too soon by mistake.' I didn't mean to sound nasty, but it came out all wrong. I was worried for a minute that I'd offended her, but that was one of the nicest things about Miranda. She didn't get upset easily. I suppose she'd had so many big things go wrong in her life that the little things didn't seem so bad. Anyway, she only laughed.

'I know what I'm doing,' she said. 'I take precautions.'

I was dying of curiosity.

'D'you mean you're on the pill or something?' I said. 'Have you really, I mean, done it, then?'

I wanted to ask her if she'd gone all the way, but I couldn't somehow bring it out. Miranda laughed and squeezed my arm.

'You've got a lot to learn, haven't you Pee-wit?' she said, and I didn't notice till afterwards that she hadn't answered my question.

'What's it like?' I said. I was desperate to know.

Miranda seemed to find it hard to put into words.

'It's just – it's cosy,' she said. That wasn't at all what I was expecting. 'When someone holds you, and you're close to them, snuggled right up, you feel all warm, and as if they loved you. Oh, I know they don't really. Boys are all the same. They just want to experiment and everything. But I don't mind if they do all that. Actually, I think it's rather boring. Overrated. I don't know what all the fuss is about. But it's so lovely having a boy have his arms round you, and tell you how nice you are, and sort of stroke you, and everything. That's what I want. That's what I like.'

Say what you liked about Miranda, she's honest. I thought a lot about what she'd said when I got home. I felt I understood her now. I could see she'd been hungry for love all her life, and now she was being offered it, a kind of love, anyway, so she was like a kid in a sweetshop, stuffing handfuls of goodies into her mouth. I'd always thought Miranda was so grown up and sophisticated, but I suddenly saw that she was really a little girl, wanting someone to cuddle her. I knew I didn't have to worry about her any more, I mean, about myself not being as experienced as her, and feeling silly and babyish and left behind. It would be different for me. Sort of holy, and wild, and all-consuming, like in *Wuthering Heights*. It wouldn't be boring for me. I felt quite sure of that.

I met Mum on the doorstep. She'd just got back from doing the shopping with Katy and Ben. I always like the days when she does a big shop at Safeways, because she can never resist the patisserie counter, and always brings back something sticky and sugary for tea. This time she had a bag of doughnuts.

'I must be crazy,' she said, smiling fondly at Ben, as he sat propped up on a cushion near the table, smearing jam and sugar all over his face, and mashing little bits of dough into the carpet.

'Who's the extra one for?' said Katy, looking at it greedily. It's so unfair the way that child pigs herself, and never seems to suffer for it. She's a perfect little fairy, Dad says, in an unusual lapse from his normal perceptive self, and she's never had a spot in her life. I should be so lucky.

'I thought Miranda might be here,' said Mum. 'She often drops in after school.' I knew she was relieved to find me alone. Mum didn't like Miranda, any more than she'd liked Debbie. I know she thought she was a bad influence on me. It got me down. She ought to have known me better, and trusted me a bit more. As if I'd start throwing myself at people, just through being friends with Miranda. I felt even more irritated now that I'd got to know her better. She needed someone like my mum to be nice to her, not to push her around.

'You're always on about Miranda,' I blurted out, knowing I was being unfair because Mum hadn't actually said a word. 'It's so mean. You don't know anything about her. She's got an awful home, and everyone's always on at her, and she needs all the friends she can get.'

Mum seemed quite startled.

'You're a loyal little soul, aren't you, Annie?' she said. For a minute, it sounded as if she was laughing at me. I knew she wasn't really, but I'd hit out before I could think.

'You're so intolerant!' I shouted. 'You don't think anyone's worth anything unless they're ordinary, and middle class, and suburban like you!'

Katy went on unpacking the shopping with a revoltingly smug look on her face. Mum was quite mild, considering.

'Come off it, love,' she said. 'I just don't want you to pick up any of Miranda's bad habits, that's all.'

I knew she was trying to be nice, but it's not easy to climb down off your high horse once you've climbed up on to it.

'How do you know,' I said cuttingly, 'that she isn't picking up any good habits from me, like loyalty, for example?' and I went out. I didn't slam the door, so Mum knew I wasn't really annoyed. Neither of us mentioned Miranda again during super, but I made a decision, a really definite decision, in the middle of the cauliflower cheese. If ever I fell in love, and had a serious boyfriend, the last place I'd take him would be home. And that would serve my mother right for being so nasty about my friends.

Thinking about boyfriends set me off thinking about Tony, of course, and I couldn't concentrate on anything much for the rest of the evening. But

later, after we'd watched a comedy show on TV, and
Katy had gone up to bed, Mum wanted to show me
how tolerant she was, so she said why didn't I invite
Miranda to help babysit for Ben while she and Dad
went round to Aunty Janice's on Saturday night. I
bet she thought she was safe. She couldn't imagine
Miranda not being booked up for a Saturday. But
when I saw Miranda on the bus next morning, she
said she'd love to come. She'd rather have a really
chatty time with me, and sit around cuddling Ben,
she said. She was off boys for the time being anyway.
So Mum got more than she bargained for. Miranda
knew quite a lot about loyalty already.

I didn't let on to Mum, but actually I was surprised
that Miranda agreed to come on Saturday. It seemed
so unlike her. She had never been known to spend
Saturday night out of male company since that time
when she was twelve, and Kevin Gallagher took her
to a party. She'd had too much to drink, and done
French kisses with Simon Petty, and on Monday
morning, at school, she'd described the whole thing,
blow by blow, in the cloakroom, while our eyes
grew rounder and rounder. Since then, Miranda's
Saturday nights had been a permanent source of
entertainment on our Monday mornings.

When I opened the door to her, the children were already in bed, and Mum and Dad had gone out. She looked unlike herself. She hadn't done herself up, and she looked much younger, and unglamorous, and as if she could be easily hurt. I nearly said straight out,

'You're not pregnant, are you?' but I managed not to.

She came in, took her shoes off straight away, and dropped down on to the sofa.

'Am I tired,' she said. 'I didn't get home till four this morning. Gary Fletcher's party.'

'What did your Dad say?' I said. 'Mine goes up in smoke if I come home late.'

'Dad!' she snorted. 'He didn't come in himself till after six. He's in love. He's got a new girlfriend, anyway.'

I couldn't think of anything to say.

'Here, Anna,' said Miranda, swivelling round on the sofa so she could look at me properly, 'have you ever been in love?'

Luckily, I had turned at that very moment to put a cassette on, and I fiddled with the knobs on the loudspeaker to give myself time. I didn't want to talk about Tony. It was the deepest secret of my life.

I felt that if I told anyone it would escape from me, and be tainted, and sullied.

'What, me?' I said at last. 'Don't be daft.'

It wasn't a lie, exactly. I've had to give up telling lies, because I can't carry it off. I look self-conscious and give the game away. Miranda didn't notice anything. She was used to me running myself down. She had only asked the question to give herself the chance to talk, anyway.

'Because I'm in love,' she said, and she threw her arms above her head, and wiggled her toes down the sofa under one of the cushions and gave a huge sigh. It's a funny thing, but during all those years that Miranda had been messing about with boys, and saying how crazy she was about Ted, or Tom, or Matthew, and swooning over their eyes, or their cool jackets, or their glitzy motorbikes, or something, I'd never once heard her actually say she was in love.

'Who with?' I said. And then all of a sudden, I was wary. I knew what she was going to say before she said it.

'Can't you guess?' She smiled up at me. Her eyes were wide open. They looked nearer without the crust of make-up that was usually caked all round them.

'You met him,' she went on. 'You know. Down at Ted's when we were all playing tennis. That wonderful tall boy with the dark hair. Tony. Come on, Anna! You remember!'

'Oh, him!' I said, and even though my throat had gone tight I managed to sound halfway normal. I couldn't look down into her face any longer without feeling like a traitor. I don't know why I felt guilty, because I hadn't done anything at all, but you can't help your feelings. I went through into the kitchen, wanting to hide my face, which I knew was going red.

'I'll get us a Coke,' I said, and clattered round, pretending to look in all the cupboards to give my face time to fade.

'Did you see him again?' I called out. It was easier to talk at a distance. 'Where did you meet him in the first place, anyway?' I waited, breathless with anxiety.

'That's the funny thing,' Miranda said. 'I'd only met him that morning. He knows Joe a bit. And I never even saw him again after that day. He went off, do you remember, when your mum arrived, and I was too thick to run after him and get his telephone number. I asked Joe about him, but he says he hasn't been around for a while, and he doesn't even know his surname, let alone where he's gone, and oh, Anna, I've never felt like this before! I'd do anything to get him. I can't be bothered to go out with all those silly little boys any more. What's the point? I keep on at Joe for his address, but he says he doesn't know anything else about him. I think he's bluffing. He's jealous, because he wants me himself. But I'll get hold of Tony if it's the last thing I do,' and she gripped a cushion between two clenched fists, and let out a sort of animal cry, then punched it furiously away from her.

My heart sank into my boots. Once Miranda had her hooks into Tony, there was no more to be said. She had a way of going after a boy that no one had ever been known to resist. She was fearless, shameless, ruthless, single-minded, and ready to do anything anyone wanted. I hadn't got a chance.

At that moment, there was a sudden wail upstairs.

'I'll go,' said Miranda, jumping up, instantly forgetting the pangs of unrequited love. 'I'll bring him down, shall I?'

'OK, if you like,' I said. Mum didn't like Ben coming down in the evening. She said it spoiled him, and he'd get into the habit, and then we'd never get him to go to sleep, but I knew Miranda was dying to cuddle him and I hadn't got the will to resist her. I was too preoccupied. My mind was spinning round, out of control, trying to grab hold of what she'd told me.

A minute later, she was downstairs again with Ben in her arms. She put him down on the sofa and let her hair flop on to his face.

'Agoo,' she said.

Ben screamed with laughter, and tried to catch hold of her hair with his little hands, but he was always just too slow as Miranda flicked it out of reach.

'Who cares about silly old boys?' she said in the special, soppy voice she always used with Ben. 'Miranda loves babies, yes she does. Miranda's going to have lots of ickle pickle babies and she's going to cuddle them all day long.'

'When you've quite finished,' I said, knowing I sounded a bit ratty, but not bothering to hide it, 'I'll give him his drink.' And I pushed her out of the way, picked Ben up off the sofa and settled him on my knee, where he drank noisily out of his cup.

Miranda might stand the best chance with Tony, but nobody would ever take Ben away from me, I thought.

Chapter Seven

Not long after the beginning of term, Ben went into hospital. He'd been in before, several times, like when they'd put a little drain thing in to take some of the fluid off his head, and when he'd had other things wrong, like bronchitis, that normal babies would have shaken off quite easily.

'Just routine,' Dr Randall said, but I didn't believe him. For one thing, Mum seemed so down about it. I caught the end of what she was saying on the phone when I got in from school.

'. . . don't think they'll operate again. It's too risky. It's the heart problem, too, I think.'

She sighed, and paused, and I could hear a sort of quacking, crackling sound which was Aunty Janice answering. Aunty Janice talks so loudly down the phone you have to hold your ear if you don't want to get your eardrums blasted.

'Oh no,' Mum went on. '*He's* not here. You might have guessed that. I sometimes think . . .' and then I saw her looking at me, and I knew she wanted to talk about Dad but wasn't going to till I was out of the way.

It was true. Dad wasn't at home much now. And it wasn't just that he went away so much, he'd sort of changed when he was home, too. When he'd first got his travelling job, it had been wonderful every time he came back. Funny, and special. Like Christmas. But that was all over now. He didn't kind of clown around any more and make a fuss of us like he used to.

I blamed Mum. She was so tight, and sort of prickly, and miserable. She'd wither him up with a look if he started messing about, and then she'd sigh and say something like,

'It's all very well you being so cheerful. You're not stuck here all the time with a sick kid and no one to talk to,' and I'd feel insulted, because she'd called me no one, and Dad would look guilty and irritated at the same time.

I hated hearing Mum going on and on about Dad to Aunty Janice. I'm never going to do that if I get married, talk about him to other people, I mean. It's sneaky. So I went into the kitchen, and made a bit of noise getting myself a cup of tea, so she'd be sort of reminded that I was there, and perhaps that might stop her being disloyal. And I was just wondering what I could do next to get her off the phone when the front doorbell rang.

The phone in our house is in the hall, right by the front door, and I heard Mum say quickly,

'Sorry, Jan, got to go,' and click the receiver down. Then I heard the door open, and Mum's voice go really polite and a bit smarmy.

'Oh hello, Mr Henderson, do come in. How nice of you to call round.'

It was the vicar.

We're not exactly what you'd call a churchy family. We only used to go at Christmas and Easter and christenings and things. But Mum had taken to going more often, and sometimes I went with her. I couldn't decide whether I liked it or not. Church made me swing violently from one mood to another. I either felt exalted and holy and full of goodwill towards men, or I was bored and grumpy and super-critical.

I didn't mind Mr Henderson usually. He was just middle-aged and ordinary. But I didn't want to see him that day, because Mum had dragged Katy and me off to the harvest festival a couple of weeks earlier, and Mr Henderson had stopped me at the church door.

'Well, well,' he'd said. 'It's Anna, isn't it?' and he'd taken my hand to shake it, and didn't seem about to let it go again. 'And how are you, young lady?'

I muttered something. I wanted to say, 'Fine thanks, old gentleman,' but of course I didn't. My life is littered with wasted opportunities. And anyway, I liked Mr Henderson.

'Have we seen you at our youth club yet?' he went on.

'No,' I said uncomfortably. I was beginning to feel trapped.

'Come next week then,' he said. I'll say one thing for him. He had the trick of speaking intensely to you as if you were all alone even though half a million people were milling round, trampling on his surplice, trying to barge in and ask him idiotic questions about choir practice, or make personal criticisms of his sermon, or moan on about what agony their piles were or something.

'What do you say, then,' he said, still gazing at me intently. 'Friday at 7.30, at the vicarage. Will you come?'

'All right,' I'd said weakly, and he'd let go my hand, and turned to the next person, and was quickly engulfed in a sea of blue rinses.

I hoped the whole thing would be quietly forgotten. The last thing I wanted to do was go to some sweaty youth club with a lot of horrible spotty kids years younger than me. So I stood in the kitchen being quiet and hoping they wouldn't come in. But of course Mum had to go and offer Mr Henderson a cup of tea, and he had to go and accept, so they both came in and caught me.

'Sorry we didn't see you on Friday,' said Mr Henderson, all bright and breezy. 'How about this week?'

'Well, I don't . . .' I mumbled, trying to edge towards the door.

'It's very kind of you to think of Anna,' said Mum with that little shrill laugh she gives when she's embarrassed. 'Of course you'll be there on Friday, won't you Anna?'

I gave her the dirtiest look I dared in front of the vicar.

'You might meet some really nice young people for a change,' said Mum, rather meaningfully.

I knew she meant 'boys' but didn't dare say so.

I could read her mind like a book. Boys at church would be safe and well-behaved and respectable, not a rough, tough lot like Miranda's.

In the end, I went. There was no way out. I might have got away with it if Mr Henderson hadn't had a surprising burst of memory for such a white-haired old gent, but he phoned Mum the next day, and said how much he was looking forward to seeing me on Friday, so that put the lid on it.

Actually, I was pleasantly surprised. I grumbled like mad about going, of course, but it wasn't at all bad. The vicarage was a funny old house with a vast basement which Mr Henderson had turned into a games room. It was really good. I'd thought it would be all holy and embarrassing, but the only holy bit was a prayer at the end, and I didn't mind that too much. Apart from that, all we did was play table tennis (and I'm brilliant at that), and Mr Henderson showed us how to score properly at darts. Most of the kids there didn't even go to church, or not much anyway. They just liked the group and Mr Henderson. There were quite a few younger ones, but they mostly watched cartoons on the video. There were several others of my age, including a girl called Diana, that I quite liked, and a boy called

Jeff who was a real comedian. He had bubbly blond hair, and a cheeky grin, and a sort of bouncy, nice, funny way of walking. When he got going doing his imitation of TV personalities, and making us guess who was who, we rolled round the floor laughing. He was brilliant at Mr Henderson. Jeff wasn't the romantic hero type, like Tony, but I could imagine myself being good friends with him. He didn't scare me. He had this fantastic knack of making really witty remarks all the time, like when Mr Henderson said, 'I don't know how you do it, Jeff, getting your Dad to lend you his car all the time. It's all right for some,' and Jeff answered, quick as a flash,

'Where there's a will there's relations.'

I could tell Jeff liked me a bit. He kept fixing it so we'd be paired off at table tennis. It was probably only because I was good at it, and it gave him a better chance of winning, but I sort of knew it was because of me, too. I was looking my best that evening, giving off the odd electric flashes, I was sure. I hadn't felt that way for ages.

I had to climb down at home, and say I quite liked youth club, and I'd go again next week. In fact, it wasn't bad to have somewhere to go on a Friday night, because for years I'd been the only girl in class, I was sure, who had nothing to do but sit at home and do even more homework, or watch boring sitcoms on TV. I'd felt a real freak, left out.

Jeff wasn't there the third time I went. Nor was Diana. I was disappointed. The sparkle had gone out of the evening. I played a bit of table tennis, and talked to a boy called Sam, but he was really boring. He'd got these red clammy hands that he kept twisting around, as if he was washing them. I was trying to shake him off when the phone rang. Mr Henderson answered it. He wrote something down on a scrap of paper.

'It's for you, Anna,' he said, handing it to me. That was just like Mr Henderson. He could have shouted out my personal business in front of everyone, and make me look an idiot, but he was wonderfully matter-of-fact and mature about it all.

The note just said, 'Anna – please meet Jeff at the station 9.30 after club.'

I couldn't believe it. A date! I felt myself going red, then shivery. Thank God I'd washed my hair before I'd gone out, and had put on my best sweatshirt. Trust Jeff to do things differently, I thought. It was such a funny way to ask me out, through Mr Henderson and everything. I hadn't realized he'd liked me that much. I hadn't realized things had gone that far. I phoned Mum, said I'd be home late, and left the club early. It was a good fifteen minute walk to the station but I wanted to have plenty of time. I had to sort things out in my mind.

It was funny, but having a real date with a real person made Tony seem further away and less interesting. I knew it would be good fun going out with Jeff. There'd be lots of laughs, and I was pretty sure we'd like doing the same kinds of things, but I could have serious conversations with him too if we both felt in the mood. I would feel a bit strange at first, because I wasn't used to going out with boys, but I wouldn't be paralysed with nerves like I would have been if Tony had asked me out. Actually, the more I thought about it, the more I liked Jeff's face better than Tony's, or what I could remember of Tony's. He was more my kind of person, somehow.

It was a funny way, though, to ask a girl out with you. I couldn't really see why he hadn't asked Mr Henderson if he could speak to me. But then I felt glad that he'd done it like this, without giving me time to think about it, or the chance to say no. I'd have got worked up into a right stew if I'd had more warning.

I hadn't been to the station in the evening very often before. It was surprisingly busy. There were a lot of people waiting, meeting friends, I suppose, or just hanging about. I was early. I couldn't see Jeff anywhere, so I stood near the do-it-yourself photo machine, and waited.

I saw him at last, after what seemed a lifetime, but was really only ten minutes. He was wearing a shabby old bomber jacket, and didn't look like his usual spruce, sparky self. He was grubby, as if he'd been doing a dirty job, and looked tired. I was just about to go up to him, when I went hot and cold all over. Diana had appeared from the other end of the entrance hall.

'Jeff!' I heard her call. He turned, and started towards her.

'Hi!' he called back. Light dawned. With a sickening thud I realized the truth. They had obviously come to meet each other. The message must have been for 'Diana', not for 'Anna'. Mr Henderson had made a ridiculous, stupid blunder. As luck would have it, I was standing right between them. They were both coming towards me. Any minute now they'd be bound to see me. I turned in panic and bolted into the photograph booth. Thank goodness, it was empty.

I heard them stop right outside, and actually saw their feet from behind the skimpy green curtain. I was nearly dying of shame. Supposing Diana recognized my shoes? She'd admired them only last week. She'd never have the chance again. I'd never have the nerve to go back to the youth club after this. I curled my feet away from the opening as far out of sight as possible.

'Glad you got my message,' Jeff was saying. He sounded rushed, and not particularly welcoming.

'Dad gave it to me,' said Diana. 'I got home late from swimming.'

'He thought you were at the youth club,' said Jeff. 'I phoned there too, and left a message for you. Funny. Mr Henderson said you were there.'

'Oh well,' said Diana. 'You know what he's like. He can be a bit vague sometimes. Let's get going. I don't want to be too late tonight. Where's the stuff?'

'It's out the back, in Dad's car,' said Jeff. 'We'll have to make a couple of journeys. I'm beginning to regret volunteering for this. I've been at it all evening. I've just about had it with jumble sales.'

Their voices moved away, and merged with the thundering of a train pounding through the station.

I sat there, quite motionless, for a good five minutes. I had never felt such a fool in all my life.

'Serves you right,' I kept saying to myself. 'Serves you bloody well right.' I don't know why I was so angry with myself. I suppose I should have blamed Mr Henderson. But it isn't easy being furious with him. Anger doesn't sort of stick to him, if you know what I mean.

It was quite a long walk home, and as I went I began to feel better. At least they hadn't seen me. And I hadn't let on to Mum. I'd just said I'd be late. The chances were that Mr Henderson wouldn't remember a thing about it. His memory, though very good in some ways, was selective. The only person who knew what a fool I was, was me. And I knew that anyway. Perhaps I would go back to the club next week, after all.

I'd learned something about myself as well. Thinking about Jeff had put Tony out of my mind, and if I could forget him so easily perhaps I wasn't in love with him at all.

Chapter Eight

The worst thing about starting a new year at school is that you always have to work a bit harder. You finish up at the end of the summer term sure that you'll die if you ever have to go through exams again, but lo and behold, come the start of autumn, there you are again. Once school had got going I found myself doing so much homework I'd have to stagger back every day, weighed down with half the school library in my bag. I never used most of the books, but I was so neurotic in case I needed to look something up and didn't have it with me, that I used to overdo it, and take far too many home just to be on the safe side. It's a wonder that I didn't end up with a permanent curvature of the spine.

Miranda didn't bother about work much, and the sickening thing was that she did nearly as well as me. She had a natural thing for languages. She could prattle away in French and German with an amazingly convincing accent, while I was still stuck, ploughing through lists of irregular verbs, and getting dreadfully muddled up with them all. Anyway, you can't really make yourself better at languages. You can either do them or you can't. But with History, and English literature, and all the stuff I cared most about, you have to wade through tons of books if you want to write a decent essay.

I'd had enough of Miranda, actually. It was mainly because she bored on and on about Tony all the time. I thought about him a lot still, in spite of the jolt I'd got when I thought Jeff was asking me out, but I knew it was unreal. I never expected to see him again. He was just the person I daydreamed about, like I used to about Miss Winter. But Miranda kept on about strategy, about how she'd hang about near the tennis courts when the good weather started again, in case he came back there, and how she'd invite him to such and such a party, or make sure her Dad was out and get him to come round to her flat. She'd have done it, too, I know she would, if Tony had shown up again. I didn't like the thought of it. If Miranda was really in love, the real thing, I mean, I didn't think she ought to stoop to sordid schemes. Her craze for Tony hadn't even stopped her carrying on with other boys. She was just the same as ever, always slipping out of school at lunchtime to meet someone down at the station snackbar. She even boasted about having an affair with a ticket collector. And she was forever mooning around with Joe in the new McDonald's that had opened up in the high street.

I didn't invite her home very often now. It wasn't only because I'd gone off her a bit. It was also because of Mum. Once Ben was back home from the hospital, she'd become more difficult than ever. Dad and I had had a very mature discussion about it on one of the weekends when he was at home. He said she was depressed, and we had to be very understanding, and she'd get better in time, and he was trying to get her to go to the doctors, but I noticed he didn't stick around to make sure she went.

To be fair, Mum had an awful lot to do with Ben. The older he got the more he needed looking after. He seemed to sleep even less at night, and he was a weight to carry round. Even ordinary things like changing his nappy and getting him up into his chair to feed him were an effort. You had to really heave to lift him off the ground. Then I suppose Mum had to keep up with the house and everything. She didn't have to do much for me, of course. Being fifteen, I was practically grown up, and less dependent on home. I could look after myself, thank you very much. But Katy still needed a lot of maternal love. I'd got quite fond of Katy, actually. She was turning out to be a rather nice person. She'd dropped a lot of her babyish ways, and was quite good company sometimes. We still had rows, of course, like when she borrowed my parrot brooch without asking me, for her school Christmas party, and it got broken when she fell off her chair in musical chairs, but on the whole, we didn't get on too badly.

Katy's birthday is in October. On October 21st in fact, the same day as Queen Victoria's, as she never fails to tell anybody who will listen. You'd have thought no one else in the world knew what birthdays are, the way Katy goes on about hers. She starts in about June every year, saying things to her friends like, 'If you don't lend me your new ballet shoes you won't be invited to my party.' It never fails.

It was that, though, which led to all the trouble. Mum came upon Katy writing out for the tenth time the list of kids she wanted to invite, crossing out Tracey because they'd had a tiff, and putting back Stewart because he'd given her a fruit gum during lunchtime, and Mum said, 'You're not expecting a party this year, are you? I couldn't possibly manage it, what with Ben being in and out of hospital and everything. Anyway, I thought you'd grown out of all that sort of thing.'

Katy couldn't believe her ears. She'd been thinking about nothing else for weeks. The fact that Mum hadn't noticed shows just how remote she had become. Everyone else was sick to death of the subject. Katy went white, then red, and shouted at Mum that she was an old cow, and ran out of the kitchen stamping up the stairs so hard that the whole house shook. I expected Mum to fly after her and give her what for. She doesn't allow language. But she just sat down at the kitchen table, and put her head in her hands. I was about to stick my oar in, and say something really cutting, because I'd had a great party when I was ten, and I thought she was being too hard on Katy, when I suddenly took pity on her. Her shoulders were drooping, and her hair looked straggly, and I could see that she was tired, all the way through, right down to her bones. So I said, and I think I was very dignified and adult about it, 'She's set her heart on it, Mum. I think, in all fairness, we'll have to do it.'

Mum didn't move. I had that awful feeling I get when the class is dead quiet, and Mrs Gordon asks for volunteers to do some poisonous job, like setting out the chairs in the hall for a parents' evening, or selling tickets for the school concert. I'm always the muggins who volunteers. I don't know why, I just seem to be propelled forward by an alien force, and before I know where I am, I'm landed with it. So I heard myself saying, without quite knowing how or why, 'You can leave the whole thing to me, Mum. I'll organize a disco for Katy, and buy in some Coke and hamburgers, and you needn't lift a finger. We'll do it next weekend when Dad's at home. He can be the disc jockey.'

She looked at me then.

'I can't stand the noise,' she said, and there was a kind of desperation in her voice, 'and kids traipsing in and out, and Ben getting out of his routine, and the mess . . .'

I started feeling annoyed then.

'Look,' I said, and I know I sounded exasperated. 'It's the kid's birthday. She's ten years old. She's told her friends. You can't let her down.'

She went on staring at me, helplessly.

'Ben can go to Aunty Janice,' I said. 'She's always offering to have him. And you can go out for the afternoon. We can manage quite well without you,' and I didn't realize until later that it must have sounded cruel.

I rather enjoyed setting up Katy's disco. For one thing, she was desperately grateful. She hung on my arm when we went down to the toy shop to choose some going-home presents. I told her she could spend two pounds on each kid, and she chose the weirdest things, like rainbow notepads, and revolting pencils with pink and yellow teddies on them. Still, I suppose a child's taste is bound to be rather naïve. I seem to remember liking the most grotesque pictures of long-eared dogs with enormous tear drops in their eyes when I was her age. She'll grow out of it one day.

I knew exactly how to organize the food. I'd had to do the hamburger and hot dog stand at the school Christmas fair. It had been a worry beforehand, but it had gone beautifully, and Miss Winter had said I had a natural talent for administration. A disco for ten little kids was a doddle in comparison with that. The hardest part, strangely enough, was persuading Dad to be a disc jockey. I never thought he'd turn funny about giving Katy a birthday party, but he seemed to think that Mum was really unwell, and that it would be too much for her, and that she needed as much peace and quiet as she could get.

'Well, why don't you stay at home a bit more,' I

burst out, 'and take the strain off her?'

Dad wasn't angry. His face just closed up and he said he didn't think he'd be of any use. He didn't seem to be able to say the right thing, ever, these days. In the end, though, he decided it might be a good idea, and he agreed to help, so we wrote six to eight on the invitations to keep it down to only two hours, and Mum said OK, but would we please make sure that the music wasn't turned up so loud that the pictures would be shaken off the walls.

I sometimes have an uncanny feeling that Katy's really the older one of us two. She's certainly got an advanced sense of fashion and style, much better than mine. I look quite good these days, though I say it myself, now that the brace is off my teeth, and I keep my lenses in all the time, and the spots are clearing up (except for the odd one on my chin). But Katy's a natural. She spends hours in front of her mirror in her room, twisting an old scarf round her head, and looking at it from all angles, or trying on different things with each other to see how they look. I must admit, she gets results. She's a ten year-old raver. I bet she'll be a model or a dress designer or something when she grows up.

She saved up weeks' worth of pocket money

before the disco and spent most of it on make-up. I wasn't sure if she should be allowed to. I mean, a ten-year-old, dolled up to the eyebrows, seems a bit obscene to me. I never even thought of it at her age. I was much too sensible.

When the day finally came, she didn't let me see her getting ready for the party. I suppose she thought I'd object. When I did see her at last, I nearly burst out laughing, which, I have learned from long experience, would have been fatal.

She was wearing a sugar-pink tracksuit, and orange Robin Hood boots, and she'd rolled a crimson scarf with lurex fringes into a rope and tied it round her forehead. So far so good. A bit on the bright side, perhaps, but within limits. But it was her make-up that knocked me out. I mean, pink and orange hair-spray in stripes (a bit wobbly down the back) and gelled so that it stuck out all over, and red eye-shadow, and black lipstick . . .

I opened my mouth, then saw the expression on her face. It was sort of hopeful, and pleading.

'You look great,' I said. 'Fantastic. Super cool.'

She did a pirouette and danced off to show Mum. And Mum actually laughed, a nice laugh, not a sarcastic one. It was such a surprise to hear it that

I knew Katy wouldn't take offence. Then I heard Mum say,

'You look wonderful, darling. However do you do it? Whatever will you think up next?' And I felt that perhaps that there was hope, that we might one day turn back into a proper, nice family again, with an ordinary Mum who did things with us.

Once Katy's friends arrived, I didn't have time to turn round, let alone notice what any of them were wearing. I began to see why Mum had made such a fuss about having the disco in the first place. The noise was horrific. Those ten kids sounded like fifty. They got so excited they shrieked for the full two hours, at the tops of their voices, almost drowning out the music which Katy had turned up as high as she dared.

I don't know, quite honestly, how much Katy enjoyed it. She seemed tense most of the time. She kept trying to organize the others into partners, and wandering into the kitchen to ask when tea would be ready, and making Dad stop the record in the middle to announce a competition for the best make-up. I think she found the whole thing a bit of a strain.

Tracey didn't help. She'd been invited after all, since she and Katy had officially been best friends for years and years, but she was mean all the time, ostentatiously ignoring Katy, and going round with Stewart, who had a slick hairstyle, and a sensational wiggle in his hips when he danced. It was Debbie and me and Emma all over again, and my heart bled for Katy. It needn't have. I've got to hand it to her, that kid's brilliant at getting what she wants. She wangled it very neatly so that Stewart sat next to her at tea, and she managed to palm Tracey off on to Conrad, a funny kid with a brush of stiff, carroty hair. Then all through tea she whispered funny, catty things to Stewart about Tracey, and Stewart laughed so much he choked on a crisp. I could see Tracey going wild with jealousy. In the end she couldn't stand it any longer, and came to try to get Stewart to dance with her again in the other room, but she timed it all wrong, because he was after a second bit of birthday cake, and Katy had promised him the slice with the most Smarties on it. So Tracey wandered off, rejected, and Katy won hands down. Good for her. I wish I'd been so clever over that sneaky Emma.

Mum stayed in bed most of the afternoon. She said she had a headache. But she popped down once or twice, and smiled at the milling mob of children. And when they'd all gone, and I'd flopped down, exhausted, on to the sofa, with empty crisp packets and birthday wrapping-paper crunching under me every time I moved, I could hear her in the kitchen with Dad.

They were in there for a long time. I thought I heard her cry, and then Dad talking softly, and then ages later, I heard them moving round, and water running and everything, and Mum's voice was louder, and natural, even happy. And I heard her laugh out loud, in a way that I hadn't heard for ages.

'Well done, Annie,' she said to me later that evening. 'You did manage without me very well. But I don't think you'll have to next time. I don't think I'm quite ready for you to take this family over yet. Especially not now Dad's going to change his job. He's putting in for a transfer so he won't have to travel so much. Think of all the shirts I'll have to iron again!' and she smiled as if she didn't know perfectly well that I knew perfectly well that she hated ironing more than anything else in the world.

Mum didn't get better overnight, but she did start being a bit more normal after that. I don't know what she and Dad had said in the kitchen, but the stupid walls they'd built up between themselves had come down again. Dad was still going to go away a lot for a couple of months, but there was light at the end of the tunnel. He'd soon be back home, and then he'd be there for good.

I don't want to boast, but I think I was the one who got it sorted out. I don't mean Dad changing his job. I think he must have decided that by himself. I mean, me doing the disco for Katy made Mum wake up to the fact that she'd got other kids besides Ben. I didn't mind her spending most of her time with him, except when she sort of squeezed me out of the way, like when he was ill and she wouldn't let anyone else cuddle him, even though I was sure he'd have preferred me sometimes. But what I did mind was that she seemed to give Katy a whole lot more time than she was prepared to give me. I know I'm too old, really, to need a mother much, but I did feel pardonably annoyed when Mum found time to take Katy ice-skating, but couldn't be bothered to go round the shops with me. It started nagging at me after a bit, and I got to the point where I noticed every tiny thing she said to Katy, and I brooded about it afterwards.

I suppose it had to boil up eventually. In the end, it was something really silly that set it off.

I was in the school play. It wasn't a speaking part or anything. I was just a guest at a party in *Lady Windermere's Fan*. I love Oscar Wilde. It makes me feel languorous, and sophisticated, and unspeakably elegant. Mrs Hamilton was directing the play, of course, and she and Miss Macfarlane, the domestic science teacher, provided the basic costume, but I had to dress it up with extras, like a collar, and costume jewellery, and long gloves and things. When Mrs Hamilton mentioned collars, I remembered Mum had a wonderful lace one tucked away in her underwear drawer. It was real, good, old lace. Her grandmother had given it to her years ago. She'd never once used it. In fact, I only knew it was there because I'd helped her tidy her drawers one day when I was off school with a cold, and I'd found it. But would she lend it me for the school play? Would she ever! It was too precious, she said. I might lose it, or cut it by mistake, or get it covered in make-up.

'Or it might get eaten by the school cat,' I said angrily. 'I do know how to take care of things, you know. Why won't you let me? It's not doing any good, mouldering away in your drawer.'

But Mum was adamant. There was nothing I could do but buy a cheap piece of broderie anglaise in Woolworth's and tack that on instead. It didn't look half so good.

And then – and *then* – the Saturday before the play, I met Katy flouncing downstairs, with Mum's best hat that she wore to cousin Julia's wedding, stuck on her head. I couldn't believe my eyes. I was cut to the heart. I pushed past Katy and tore up to Mum's bedroom. She was tidying out her wardrobe.

'It's not fair,' I yelled at her. 'Katy gets whatever she wants. She's only got to lift a finger. But I want something for serious educational purposes and you couldn't care less. I've had enough. I'm taking it, whatever you say,' and I darted over to Mum's chest of drawers, and wrenched open the drawer, and dragged out the collar and stood there, glaring at her, my chest heaving with emotion, and, I felt quite sure, my eyes flashing magnificently.

'Put it down at once,' my mother said sharply, and I could see that she was really annoyed.

'Why should I?' I said. 'You've given Katy your best hat just to play with.'

I saw light dawn in Mum's face, and the anger melted out of it.

'Annie,' she said, in her irritatingly understanding voice. 'Do you know how much that collar is worth?'

'No,' I said, feeling suddenly unsure of myself. I had never thought of it as having a value, in money I mean.

'At least a hundred and fifty pounds,' she said, 'unless you've just torn it.'

'What?' I gasped. I suddenly felt as if the thing in my hands was red hot. I put it gently down on her dressing table.

'Why didn't you tell me before?' I said. 'I'm quite capable of understanding things, you know, if they're properly explained to me.'

'I know, darling,' she said, and I heard a hint of laughter in her voice. I suppose I did sound rather funny. Wounded dignity, sort of thing.

'Well anyway,' I said, feeling on safer ground, 'I still don't see why Katy should have your best hat.' She laughed out loud at that.

'Best?' she said. 'Have you looked at it lately? It's got a hole the size of a 10p piece in the brim. It's not exactly new, you know. Julia's been married for five years. They've got two children already. Anyway, I shan't need a hat for years. The next wedding I go to will probably be yours.'

'Don't be silly, Mum,' I said. 'No one will ever want to marry me.'

'Oh yes, they will,' she said. 'I've noticed lately that you're looking very pretty these days. I've been turning out some materials this afternoon. I thought you might like me to make you a dress.'

It was a nice thought of Mum's and I appreciated the offer, but I was slightly taken aback at the same time. Mum can get very enthusiastic about sewing when she gets going, which isn't very often, but the results are patchy, to say the least. Occasionally she produces a real knock-out, but more often than not, it doesn't fit, and the seams are a bit ruckled, and the hem wobbles up and down. I looked at the materials she'd dug out. They were all several years old, and in colours that no one would be seen dead in now. But I was so happy I didn't care. Mum wanted to make me something. Mum thought I was pretty. Ben and Katy weren't the only ones Mum loved.

'And anyway,' I said to myself afterwards, when I had time to think, 'I don't have to wear it very often.'

I made a sudden decision. It was time I got a Saturday job. Emma and Vicky were both working at Tesco's at the weekend. I could do the same. I could start making some real money myself, and then I'd be able to buy my own clothes for a change.

Chapter Nine

In the end, I didn't get a job at Tesco's. They told me they were full up. I think Emma sabotaged my chances, actually. She shrieked when she saw me coming for an interview, and said, right in front of the supervisor, 'Oh look! It's Pea-brain! Don't worry, Pea-brain, we won't let on. We won't tell them the truth about you. Ha ha!' and then she dug Vicky in the ribs. The supervisor turned round and gave me a dirty look, and was very stiff and starchy in the interview. I knew I wasn't going to get in before she even told me. Vicky didn't help. She just smirked. I didn't blame her though. She's so used to being on the receiving end of Emma's nastiness, I suppose it made a change to be ganging up with her on someone else. But I could have strangled Emma. There are no limits to that girl's malice.

I went off home, and stopped at Mrs Chapman's to get a packet of envelopes. I felt sure I was going to have to write a lot of applications. But there was a lovely surprise waiting for me.

'Writing love letters, I suppose?' said Mrs Chapman, nodding and winking at me so that her double chins bounced up and down as she took my money. You mind when some people tease you, but you'd never mind with Mrs Chapman. She's got such a nice nature herself she only laughs if anyone takes the mickey out of her, and her attitude sort of rubs off on to other people.

'Funny kind of love letters,' I said. 'I'm looking for a Saturday job. I'm going to write off to a few places.'

'You want to work Saturdays?' said Mrs Chapman. She looked thoughtful.

'Yes,' I said. 'Half the girls at school do, and I fancy having some money of my own for a change. I'd like to get myself a few things to wear, and save up for when I go skiing with the school next year.'

'Where are they working, then, your friends?' said Mrs Chapman.

'Oh, just Tesco's, and McDonald's, and the garden centre down Stack's Lane,' I said.

'How much do you get in Tesco's?' she asked.

I told her.

'That's fair,' she said. 'Look, Anna, why don't

you work for me? I'll give you the same. I could use some help Saturdays. It's always busy in here. My poor old legs kill me, what with jumping up and down every five minutes to get something off the high shelves. I can't get around like I used to.'

I couldn't believe it.

'You don't mean it, do you, Mrs Chapman?' I said. 'You can't be serious?'

" 'Course I'm serious,' she said. 'I wouldn't joke about something like that. When do you want to start? Now?'

'I'd better just pop home and tell Mum,' I said. 'She's expecting me back at lunchtime.'

'Give her a ring,' said Mrs Chapman. 'There's a phone through the back there,' and she lifted up the flap in the counter, and stood back to let me through.

I've been going into that shop ever since I can remember, but never, not in my wildest dreams, did I imagine that I'd be allowed past the counter, under the magic flap, to see the mysteries behind. It's funny, when you think about it, how many things in this life you never notice. I mean, I've been walking down our high street for years, but I never looked up above the shop fronts till the other day. I was quite surprised. The buildings were interesting, all in different styles, and some had windows with proper curtains, and window boxes full of flowers on the sills. I suppose they must be flats. I'd always thought the high street was just shops. After that I noticed front doors squeezed in between the shop fronts. I must have been blind as a bat not to notice them before.

It was nice in behind Mrs Chapman's. She had a sort of sitting room cum storeroom, with a few comfy chairs, a gas fire, a place to make tea, and a lot of boxes full of Bounty Bars and things. I'd never thought of her as living anywhere, really. She just seemed to belong behind her counter, but she told me later that she had a nice bungalow on the main road, handy for the buses.

I felt nervous, that first Saturday morning, standing behind the counter. Fortunately, I'd been in the shop so often I knew where most things were. Mrs Chapman gave me a blue checked nylon overall to wear, and it's funny, but once I had it on, I felt official, and in charge. The customers treated me differently too. Most people didn't look at me properly, I mean as myself, Anna Peacock. They saw my overall, realized I was an assistant, and stared through me or past me. It was, 'Couple of packets of plain crisps and a *TV Times* please,' or, 'Is this week's *Woman* in yet?'

You had to have a lot of patience. I remember thinking years ago that you had to have a butterfly mind to work in a shop. I don't think that anymore. You just need to be able to keep your temper, have a good pair of legs, and eyes in the back of your head.

I got annoyed with the children sometimes. They were so noisy, and pushy, never letting anyone else get near the counter. And they'd stand there, with 10p in their hands, taking half an hour to choose one chocolate bar, making you tell them the prices over and over again. Mrs Chapman was ever so good with them. I tried to be. She told me I'd been just the same when I was a kid. She could see me now, weighing up whether to spend my pocket money on a bouncy rubber ball or a stick of liquorice as if my life depended on it. I don't believe I was as bad as those kids, though. For one thing, I was never that cheeky.

Some of the old people were nice. They tended to notice me more, and be polite. They liked to stop for a chat. But there were a few that needed careful handling. One old lady came in to buy a birthday card for her brother. Mrs Chapman gave me a little shove towards the card rack when she saw her coming.

'You'd better go and give her a hand,' she whispered. 'Poor old girl's often in here. She doesn't know the time of day no more.'

She was right.

'I'm looking for a birthday card,' the old lady said brightly, 'for my brother.' She'd pulled a card out of the rack already. It said 'For a boy who's seven' on it.

'How old is your brother?' I said.

'That's none of your business,' she snapped. I looked round at Mrs Chapman. I was beginning to feel out of my depth. But she was busy selling bubblegum to a couple of eight-year-old toughies.

'Does he like the countryside?' I said, showing her a nice scene of fields and trees, with a thatched cottage in the foreground. She started hunting round in her handbag for her glasses. She'd forgotten the card she was holding. It fluttered to the ground. I picked it up.

'That's right,' she said. 'Drop everything on the floor. You need to be a bit more careful.'

I decided to be ruthless.

'That's a nice card you've chosen,' I said, putting

the one I'd picked out in her hands. 'Is it for anyone special?'

'Yes, it's for my brother,' she said, suddenly all smiles.

'That's nice,' I said, leading her up to the till. 'It's his birthday, is it?'

'Yes.' She leaned forward confidentially. 'You'll never guess how old he is.'

'No,' I said. 'I'm sure I wouldn't.'

'Eighty-one!' she said triumphantly, as I took a coin out of the open purse she held out towards me, and put the change back into it. It's a good thing I'm honest. I could have helped myself to her old-age pension and she'd never have known the difference.

I got the giggles then. I had to turn away so she wouldn't see. But when she'd got herself out of the shop, Mrs Chapman turned on me.

'That's enough,' she said sharply. I'd never heard her speak like that before. 'I won't have you laughing at Miss Baggs, poor old lady. She used to be a music teacher. Highly respected. Spent years and years teaching snotty kids to play the piano. It's not her fault her memory's slipped a bit. She's a fine old lady. So don't let me catch you laughing at her again, mind.'

I felt bad for a few minutes, but the shop was full, and by the time we'd served everyone, Mrs Chapman was smiling and good-humoured again. She was like that, Mrs Chapman was. She never stayed cross for more than a minute at a time. And another thing I liked about her was that she had a lot of respect for people, even for old dears like Miss Baggs, who, say what you like, is as nutty as a fruitcake. Now I come to think about it, she even had respect for Ben.

By the middle of the afternoon my feet were like a couple of minced hamburgers. I'd got on these lovely shoes with red clip-on bows and high heels that I'd bought cheap in the sale. They were a bit pinched round the toes, but I usually wore them when I was out because they looked so nice, and I suppose you have to suffer a bit for the sake of beauty. But after a few hours, my toes were killing me. I kicked the shoes off when I was behind the counter, but I could never spend long enough there for them to recover, because Mrs Chapman kept saying, 'Fetch me down another box of balloons from the top shelf, will you, Anna?' or, 'Pop out to the front and tidy up the magazine rack. It looks as if a bomb's hit it.'

I could see why she needed an assistant. I don't know how she'd managed so long on her own. To

reach the top shelves she had to stand on a little pair
of steps, and I thought she'd wobble off more than
once, she was so big, and sort of stiff in her legs, and
the joints of the steps were tired. But that made it all
the nicer, working for her. I knew I was being really
useful, really earning my money.

I was beginning to feel that I'd been there for
ever, and could run the shop single-handed, when
I had a shock. A posh woman in a fur coat and one
of those expensive Hermes scarves with horses'
heads and hooves and saddles all over it came up
to the counter and bought a fistful of expensive
magazines, like *Vogue* and *Harpers* and *Interiors*. I had
never imagined that people, ordinary people I mean,
actually bought that kind of thing. I'd only seen them
in the dentist's waiting room. Anyway, this woman
had such a plummy accent I could hardly understand
a word she said, and she had a sort of haughty way
of looking at you down her long, powdered nose. I
was idly watching her as she went down the shop on
the way out, and she stopped at the pen rack, and
then, cool as a cucumber, she lifted a biro out of the
rack, slipped it into her pocket and walked out, bold
as brass.

I couldn't believe my eyes. I was sort of frozen

with shock. I knew I should have run after her, and told her to put it back, but her superior manner had made me kind of freeze up.

'Mrs Chapman, that woman – the biro,' I said incoherently.

'What's the matter, love?' said Mrs Chapman, bending down with a creaking noise to rub the corn on her foot.

'That woman, in the fur coat, she stole a biro. I saw her. She just lifted it out of the rack and put it in her pocket.'

To my surprise, Mrs Chapman laughed.

'Oh, that must have been Mrs Thompson,' she said. 'She's a shocker. Got a reputation for it. She only does it when her husband's at home. He works out in the Middle East somewhere. Makes pots of money, he does, and when he comes home he gives her hell. She goes a bit barmy. You'd never think she was a thief, dressed up to the nines like she is, and all. She got had up once. Mr Featherstone, round the corner in the grocer's, he caught her red-handed with some fancy biscuits. He doesn't hold with shoplifting. It makes him see red. So he wouldn't take an apology or anything, and he called the police. She had to go to court, and stand in the dock and everything. Got off with a fine, though. Didn't have to do time, like most people. She was nice about it afterwards. She came round and apologized to all the shopkeepers on the parade. Half of us had no idea what she'd been up to. She said she didn't know what came over her, and would I keep an eye on her, and chalk up anything else she pinched on her newspaper bill. I'll say one thing for her, she never takes anything worth more than a few pence. And she gives me a whacking great Christmas box. More than makes up for the stuff she gets away with, I'm sure. What kind of biro was it now? Fancy or plain?'

You certainly see life in a newsagent's. I'd never have thought it. I'd never have imagined that someone like Mrs Thompson, so grand, and rich, and respectable looking, would be a thief.

I felt great that evening, going home with money in my pocket. It was a landmark in my life. I would have skipped down the road if I'd been a few years younger, and my feet hadn't been killing me. I could imagine myself in a few years' time, being independent, and on my own, leading my own life, earning my own money. I made great plans for saving up, and opening a bank account, and getting one of those stunning all-in radio cassette players.

But then I passed the cake shop.

That cake shop's been there ever since I can remember. It calls itself a continental patisserie, but there's nothing foreign about the doughnuts and apple slices and cream horns that load the shelves and make you stop every time you pass the window. Every day, they display a big cake, as a sort of centrepiece. When I was little, it was my dream that one day I'd march in, and point to the window, and say, very coolly,

'I'll have the big one, please, in the middle.'

That day, the centre cake was a chocolate one with whipped cream piped round the top, decorated with flaky almonds. I don't honestly know what came over me. A sort of rush of blood to the head, I suppose, or rather, to the heels, because they seemed to turn of their own accord, and walk into the shop, and before I knew what had happened, I was back outside again, with a large box in my hands. I felt a bit of a fool then. There was too much for the five of us, even though Dad was at home for once, because Mum usually did a fry-up on Saturday nights, which didn't leave any room for afters. But so what? I knew Ben would love it. I could just picture him, smearing it all over his face, and then licking his fingers with a sort of astonished look in his eyes, as if he'd made a fantastic new discovery. And anyway, I felt like celebrating. I wanted them all to realize that I'd stepped a bit further on in my life.

It's surprising how quickly new things become routine. After only a few Saturdays at Mrs Chapman's I felt I'd worked there for years. It was tiring at first. I had to think all the time about where to find things, and about how much change to give, and I always had to look at the prices on every item instead of just ringing them up on the till, like Mrs Chapman could. The first couple of weeks I went home exhausted, and flopped into bed early on Saturday night, when Miranda was just beginning her nightly round, and slept in most of Sunday morning, testing my legs gingerly under the blankets whenever I half woke up to see how stiff they were. At least after that first Saturday I'd learned my lesson about shoes. I wore my oldest, flattest and most comfortable, and couldn't have cared less how I looked.

Once I got used to it, though, I could have done the job with my eyes shut. Mrs Chapman was lovely to work for. I did my best for her because I liked her so much, and I could see she really needed the help, but she was easygoing, and appreciated anything I did that she hadn't asked me to do. I took quite a pride in the shop, as if it was my own, and I liked sorting out little corners for her, that had lain undisturbed for years. I stopped telling Mum about it after she wanted to know why I couldn't do the same in my bedroom, but it wasn't the same at all. She couldn't see that. Mrs Chapman gave me a bonus, sometimes, if I did something extra, like mucking out the mess under the counter, or cleaning out the window and putting the display back properly. Perhaps if Mum had learned about bonuses things might have been different at home.

It was the second Saturday in November when the phone in the back room suddenly rang. Mrs Chapman was unpacking a load of early Christmas cards in there, so she answered it. I heard her say,

'Oh yes, hello, Mrs Peacock,' and then there was a silence while Mum was obviously speaking at the other end. And then Mrs Chapman said, 'That's all right. I quite understand. Do you want to speak to her yourself, or shall I give her the message?' Then there was another long pause, and she said, 'Don't worry, we're quiet in here today. She'll be with you in a few minutes.'

'Ben,' I thought. 'Something's happened.' But Mrs Chapman didn't look upset or anything as she manoeuvred her way through the small space between the stacks of newspapers that stood in the doorway of the back room.

'That was your mum,' she said. 'You'll have to hop along home. She's got to take Ben down for his appointment at the hospital, and your sister's gone down with something. Temperature's way up, and she's very poorly. Your mum wants you to look after her.'

She must have seen the face I pulled, because she gave one of her wheezy chuckles.

'Price of popularity, dear,' she said. 'Everyone seems to want you today.'

Chapter Ten

Katy had flu. At least, that's what Mum called it. The doctor said it was a virus. He always says that. It doesn't matter if you've gone blue with green spots, and your head's bursting, and your cough is like Krakatoa erupting, you've still only got a virus, and all he can do is tell you to keep warm and drink plenty of fluids. I prefer illnesses with proper names, like chickenpox, or mumps. At least you know then what you're in for.

I got it next. I had a temperature, and I felt rotten for a day or two, but I wasn't as bad as Katy. I only spent a day in bed, and then I mooned round downstairs, in the sitting room mainly, trying to summon up the energy to finish my tapestry kit of a couple of ponies that Aunty Janice had given me for my birthday. Aunty Janice didn't realize, but I wasn't that keen on ponies. She'd been mad about them at my age, so she expected me to be, too. It was too late to explain to her. She'd given me too many horsy presents already. Anyway, I'd done the interesting bits, and there were only acres of boring background left, so I couldn't be bothered to do any more. I just lay on the sofa, reading a novel, minding Ben while Mum got on with housework upstairs.

We've got a bookcase in our sitting room. It's got paperbacks on the top shelf, the Bible, Shakespeare and dictionaries on the middle shelf, as well as a couple of ornaments, and some big heavy books on the bottom, things like *The Country Diary of an Edwardian Lady*, and the *Vogue Book of Fashion*, that Granny picks up cheap in cut-price bookshops and gives Mum for her birthday. Most of the big books have brightly coloured covers, and are shiny and eye-catching. I suppose that's why Ben could never leave them alone.

He'd learned to move about at long last or at least, to sort of roll himself along the floor. I suppose he'd have found his big head too hard to control if he'd tried to get about on his hands and knees. It was difficult to see exactly how he did it, but one moment he'd be chewing the edge of the curtain, and the next moment he'd be over the other side of the room, half inside the cupboard. Most children of his age, of course, would have been walking for a long time, but he could get about surprisingly fast, especially on the vinyl floor in the kitchen. Carpet slowed him down a bit. Surface tension or something, I suppose.

Anyway, that morning, I was so busy reading my novel I'd forgotten about Ben. I'd got to the bit where the miner's daughter had run away to London on the stagecoach, and was roaming the streets in search of honest lodging, a prey to the lust and depravity of dissolute aristocrats and heartless footpads. I love historical novels. You can daydream better. Everything seems more dramatic, and beautiful, and highly coloured, like in the theatre.

I was jerked out of my book by a sudden crash. Ben had pulled half the books out of the bottom shelf.

'No!' I said, loudly.

He jumped, startled, then he looked round at me. His chin wobbled, and I thought he was going to cry, but then a sort of interested, curious look flitted across his face. His hand reached out again to the next book.

'No, Ben,' I said. 'Naughty. Stop it.'

His eyes danced, and a grin, a purely cheeky, wicked grin spread over his face, and he rolled down the bookshelf a bit further, and reached up, looking round at me, waiting for me to say no.

'No, Ben,' I said, trying not to smile. 'No!'

He stopped, put his hands over his eyes and peeped at me through his fingers, chuckling with pleasure. Whatever else he hadn't got, Ben certainly had a sense of humour.

I knew that once he'd started, he'd go on playing his little game for hours, and I didn't feel up to responding to him, so I tidied up the bookshelf, fetched him a rusk from the kitchen, and pushed some chairs in front of the bookshelves so he couldn't get at them again. He settled down quickly, sucking on his rusk, and pushing his fluffy rabbit in and out of the waste paper basket, and I went back to my book. If only I'd known, if only I'd realized, I'd have played with him all day, as long as he wanted, as long as he could.

I slept that afternoon, and when I woke up I heard Ben grizzling. He went on and on, and I couldn't hear Mum. I thought she might have popped out for a minute, so I went to see what the matter was. Mum was there. She was sitting in her favourite armchair with Ben on her knee, trying to give him a drink. He looked hot and flushed, and kept pushing the beaker away.

'He's got it,' Mum said. 'I knew he would. The doctor says to keep him warm and give him plenty to drink. More bad nights, I suppose. Pity your father's always away at exactly the wrong moment.'

Ben was bad in the evening. He tossed about, and moaned, and his temperature was way up. I didn't take much notice. He'd been this bad before. Katy had seemed much worse, the first night she'd had it, and two days later she was bouncing round again, dressing herself up in Mum's old clothes and yelling, 'Look! *Look* at me, Anna! Don't you think I'm like Princess Di?'

Mum gave Ben some Junior Paracetamol in the end, and he quietened down a bit. Then she went to get his cot ready, and gave him to me to hold, and I sang to him. He always loved singing. He knew 'The Teddy Bears' Picnic', and 'Hark the Herald Angels', and 'Happy Birthday to You'. He could even beat time perfectly. I rocked him gently while I sang, and the beating slowly stopped, and his head fell back on my shoulder. He was asleep. Mum came then, and took him out of my arms, and up to his little bed, all soft and fleecy, and baby warm.

*

I think it was Ben's bedroom door banging shut that roused me, without really waking me up. I half heard Mum's feet pattering down the stairs, and the buttons on the telephone clicking as she pressed the numbers. Then her voice, high and desperately afraid, came floating into my mind, and merged with a dream of hospitals, and a memory of Ben's birth.

'Dr Randall? It's Mrs Peacock here. I'm sorry to call you in the night, but it's Ben. He's not breathing right, and I can't rouse him. Please, oh can you . . . I'm so worried . . . No, my husband's away at the moment. I'm on my own. Oh thank you, Dr Randall. Fifteen minutes, you said?'

The receiver clicked down again, and she ran back upstairs and into Ben's room. I slipped back again into a deep sleep, as reality and the dream melted into nothingness.

It was probably the cough mixture Mum had given me that knocked me out completely that night. I didn't hear the doctor coming, or the sound of him working over Ben's cot, or Mum's frantic telephone calls to the hotel up north where Dad was staying, or her first expressions of grief. I knew nothing till 6 o'clock in the morning, when she crept into my room, and lay down beside me on my bed, and burst into a storm of tears.

She didn't have to tell me what she was crying for. I had woken with a lead weight pressing down on my heart. I knew for sure that Ben was dead, as if God himself had told me. I couldn't cry. I lay there, rigid and dry-eyed, frozen with shock. I couldn't remember his name. I couldn't remember what he looked like. I wondered who this strange woman was, who had come into my room, and was lying on my bed. One word hammered away in my mind, blocking out everything else:

'No! No! No!'

A sound made me look up. Katy stood in the door, her eyes wide, her mouth trembling.

'What is it?' she said. 'Why's Mum crying?'

Mum sat up then, and put her arms out. Katy went into them. She was crying in sympathy before she'd even heard what had happened.

'Ben's been very ill,' Mum said.

A wild, insane joy surged through me. Had I misunderstood? Was there still hope? Katy waited, passively, to be told more. I waited, my heart in my mouth, to hear what I already knew.

'He's gone,' said Mum. 'He's passed away in the night.'

'What do you mean?' said Katy. There was no point in trying to break it gently. Katy had to have everything spelled out to her, in black and white. I heard my own voice, sounding dry and harsh.

'She means he's dead,' I said.

Katy burst at once into loud, easy sobs. She sat on Mum's knee and tried idiotically to comfort her.

'You've still got me,' she said. 'And Anna,' she added as an afterthought. 'Don't cry Mum. I can't bear it. Please don't cry.'

The doorbell rang. Mum lifted her head.

'That'll be the nurse,' she said. 'Stay in here, you two. I'll go. Please stay in here. Anna, make sure Katy . . .' I nodded at her, and she left the room.

Katy went on sobbing for a while but with less and less conviction. I could see she thought that crying was the correct thing to do, but I knew she was feeling excited as much as anything, and full of curiosity.

'Why aren't you crying, Anna?' she said at last. 'Don't you care?'

I took no notice. It wasn't worth bothering to answer. Ben had never been hers in the way he'd been mine. Anyway, I couldn't have spoken to anyone just then. I heard the tap running in the bathroom, and a firm tread in the hall outside, and a soothing, unfamiliar female voice. And then at last steps went down the stairs, and Mum came into my room.

'Come down now,' she said, 'and eat your breakfast. Dad should be here soon.'

Breakfast was a disgusting idea. The thought of food revolted me. But it was the next thing to do. You get up, you get dressed, then you have your breakfast. Even when there's a death in the house, that's what you do. If you stop doing that, life stops altogether. I managed to drink a cup of tea, and pretended to have some toast. Katy ate a full bowl of cornflakes and asked for more. I had to keep telling myself that she was only ten.

Mum went to the telephone then, and I heard her speak to Granny, and then she went to her room, and I went to mine. The house was uncannily silent and quiet.

'This is what it's going to be like,' I thought. 'We'll miss the sound of him first.'

I opened my door, and went quietly along to Ben's room, and slipped inside. The curtains had been drawn, and there was only a dim light coming into the room.

The nurse had moved the cot. It was in the wrong

place, alone, in the middle of the room, where he couldn't see the pigeons who were already pecking on the window sill.

'I'll put it right for you,' I whispered, and I pushed it back into place. Then I looked at him.

He was the same. He was himself, asleep. The bedclothes were unnaturally tidy, that was all. One hand lay outside the coverlet, the little fingers curled up, relaxed. The nurse had brushed his hair, and his curls lay smooth as cream silk against his big, blue-veined head.

'Respiratory failure,' Mum had said, on the phone to Granny. I'd been afraid that he would look anguished, choking for breath, in pain, but he didn't. Just restful, and quiet, and happy.

My foot kicked against something soft. It was his fluffy rabbit. I picked it up, and tucked it down beside him.

'There you are,' I said. 'There's rabbit.'

My hand brushed against his face. It was cold, quite cold. I knew then. I couldn't pretend any more that he would wake up in a minute, and put out his arms, asking to be lifted. That was the moment when I believed that he was dead. But I knew, even then, that he was still with me, still near, still loving me.

His spirit hadn't quite gone away. It lingered on like a perfume when its wearer has just left the room.

I knelt down then, on the floor beside the cot, and stroked his hand gently, because I was afraid I might disturb him. I talked to him. I told him things. I told him what had happened when I'd first seen him, and how I'd loved him straight away. I told him that he was the best kind of brother and that I'd never wanted him to be different. I told him I'd go on loving him for ever, as long as I lived. I told him he'd be all right.

And then I kissed him, to say goodbye, and the frozen lump in my chest started to melt, and I ran out of his room, and flung myself down on my bed. That's where Dad came to me, later. And when I saw him I found at last that I could cry, and I couldn't stop, and we cried together until there were no tears left.

Chapter Eleven

I don't know if you've ever been to a funeral. If you haven't, you probably think they're morbid and creepy. But if you've been to the funeral of someone you loved, you probably found, like I did, that it was a help. It was like having a nurse wash a nasty wound and put a plaster on it. You dread her touching it, and it hurts a lot at the time, but it's better afterwards.

It was the days before the funeral that were so horrible. We lived in a peculiar limbo, with cards and letters arriving, and Mum and Dad always on the telephone, and all the time I was thinking about Ben, lying in the undertaker's chapel, a couple of miles away.

Then there was school. Dad phoned Mrs Gordon, and she told the class, so I didn't actually have to break the news, but I had to face everyone's sympathy. I could see that they were embarrassed and didn't know what to say. They either treated me like an invalid, too delicate to bear the slightest loud noise or sudden movement, and talked to me in hushed tones, being hideously tactful, or they avoided me altogether. I saw Sandra actually turn and double back down the corridor that ran alongside the gym when she saw me at the other end. She was great at battering a hockey ball through a solid line of hearty defenders, but give her a human problem and she went to pieces. I expected Miranda to understand, but she'd gone and caught the virus. She sent me a note, which made me cry, and I could see she felt miserable about Ben. She'd loved him a lot. But it was Debbie, unpredictable, self-controlled Debbie, who really surprised me.

'There's no point in pretending I know how you feel,' she said bluntly, as we sat on the radiator by the window, waiting for Mrs Hamilton to turn up for English, 'because nothing so awful has ever happened to me. I don't even know what to say, or whether you want to talk about it. Well? Do you want to?'

It was lovely to be with someone straightforward. Debbie didn't deal in evasions. She bludgeoned straight through to the heart of the matter, brushing aside obstacles with a swish of her beautiful hair, and she couldn't understand why other people didn't do the same.

'Tell me what happened,' she said. 'Were you with him all the time? Did he cry a lot? Did it hurt?'

I began to talk then, answering her hesitantly at first, and then going on and on, until I was pouring everything out, breaking off to borrow her tissues when I cried, going over his last day, and the dreadful morning when it had happened. I hardly noticed that the rest of the class had fallen silent, and that they'd gathered round to listen. I didn't mind. I wanted to talk and talk. I found myself repeating things over and over again.

'Why?' I kept saying. 'Why did he have to be born like that? It's so unfair. Why did he have to die? What was God thinking about, making a child suffer like that? Where was God when he died?'

My questions hung in the air. Not even Debbie tried to answer. I could see prissy Lucy screwing up her face and trying to fish out a quote from the Bible to throw at me. She's very religious, and thinks she knows all the answers. But then Mrs Hamilton's rich, deep voice suddenly broke in. She must have been standing at the back of the group listening.

'Even such is Time, that takes in trust
Our youth, our joys, our all we have,
And pays us but with earth and dust.'

Trust her to have a poem ready on the tip of her tongue.

'Come on, everyone,' she said. 'Get back to your places. Anna's asked some very important questions, and we're going to discuss them.'

I was furious with her. I felt she was taking my feelings away from me and exploiting them for her silly English lesson. But it didn't work out like that. It was really good. If Mrs Hamilton never makes it as an actress, she'll still have a great future on TV doing one of those discussion shows, where they invite people who wildly disagree with each other, and someone has to sit in the middle and sort of conduct it all.

After that, school was all right. It didn't exactly get back to normal, but the ice was broken. It was much harder at home. Mum was up and down like a see-saw, sometimes talking non-stop to whoever would listen to her, in a way that was quite unlike her, and then clamming up and going to her bedroom, and not answering even the simplest questions. The neighbours weren't much help. They were mostly like the girls had been at school, too embarrassed to say anything, and keeping out of our way. Mrs Russell from next door tried to be nice. She brought in little presents, a bunch of flowers, or a tin of home-made flapjacks. It wasn't the presents so much as the feeling that she was thinking of us in a kind way. But then she messed it up by saying to Mum, 'You'll soon get over it. It's a blessed release, really, isn't it?'

Mum was really mad with her. She'd said to Granny herself, I'd heard her, that at least Ben had been released from a lot of suffering, but she didn't like anyone else saying it. And she knew, we all knew, that we'd never get over it. You never get over some things. You just learn to live with them. Mrs Russell made it even worse by going on and on about how she understood, because her husband had died last year, and she talked about it non-stop, and you couldn't help feeling that she was only coming round all the time because she was lonely, and wanted us to sympathize with her. She'd get off the subject of Ben as soon as it came up, and get back on to the subject of her Percy.

Katy didn't help. She veered from being moody

and tearful, to being horribly bright and cute and little girl-y, trying to get everyone's attention. I hadn't got any patience with her at all. But two days before the funeral, I found her sitting in her wardrobe, where she often goes if she's upset, and she looked so still and woebegone that I felt sorry for her.

'What's the matter with you?' I said.

She said nothing, but held up a little china bambi that Granny had given her when she was three. It was her dearest possession. She always said that if there was a fire and she only had time to grab one thing, she'd go for her bambi.

'What's happened to it?' I said. 'Have you broken it or something?'

She shook her head, so I sat down on the floor and waited. Katy always tells you things in the end. You just have to give her time. She's the sort who can never keep anything secret. Not like me. I often imagine I'm being tortured, and that I'm not telling the names of my fellow revolutionaries. I know I'd be able to keep my trap shut. It's one of my greatest talents.

I got it out of Katy quite quickly. She was feeling awful, because she'd never let Ben touch bambi and he'd often wanted to. He used to point to it, and grizzle, and she'd always snatched it out of reach and run off. Sometimes she'd even teased him with it to make him cry. But now she was so sorry, and she felt so bad about it, and she wanted to give bambi to Ben to take with him. I was shocked at that. It didn't seem decent to me. But then Katy started to cry, and once she started she couldn't stop, and then Dad came in, and asked what the fuss was all about. So I explained it, and he thought for a bit, and then to my surprise, he took Katy's part. He said it was a very nice idea, and he would take her to the undertakers that afternoon, and she could see Ben in the chapel there.

Dad has never been known to refuse Katy anything, at least, not that I can think of. It's the worst thing about him. I don't know why I said I wanted to go too. I suppose it was because I was restless, and thinking about Ben all the time, and I felt drawn to him, as if there was a piece of elastic pulling me.

I hadn't realized that the coffin would be so small, lying there on a big table, in the chapel of rest. It was white, with silver handles, and when Mr Roberts, the undertaker, opened it, and put back the lid, I saw that it was lined with white satin. I felt good about that. It was like a little cot, cosy and comfortable. I looked down at Ben, expecting him to be the same as when I'd seen him last, but he wasn't. He looked kind of pinched, and waxen. But the real change was that now I could see he had gone. His spirit was no longer there, hovering like an invisible sweetness in the air. It had flown away. It was only his shell left in the box, as meaningless now as the chrysalis which the butterfly sloughs off. I was grateful to Katy. I was glad I'd seen him again. I put my arm around her as we looked down at him together. She snuggled into me. I'd hardly ever cuddled her, but I enjoyed it. I felt a rush of affection for her. She looked up at me.

'I'm the youngest now, aren't I, Anna?' she said. I realized then that it had been tough for Katy too. Ben had robbed her of her Mum for two years of her childhood. He'd taken me away too. I'd had no time for her while he had been alive. I gave her shoulders a squeeze.

'Go on then,' I said. 'Where's bambi?'

She pulled it out from under her sweatshirt, gave it a last kiss, stroked its glazed back, and put it down beside Ben.

'Do you think he knows?' she said.

'Yes, of course he does,' I said, and the extraordinary thing was, I felt absolutely sure about it. 'He knows, and he's really pleased, and it was a very nice thing to do.'

The day of the funeral was bright and sunny. It was one of those days in early winter when everything is golden and glowing; and scarlet berries, huge spiders' webs, curled yellow leaves and bulbous brown seed heads make sort of still-life pictures everywhere you look. It seemed all wrong to me. I'd imagined the funeral on a dark and gloomy day, with dripping trees, and mist.

It started off badly. I wanted to wear something black, or at least as dark as possible. I chose my clothes carefully. Dad said most people didn't bother with mourning nowadays, but I wanted to wear it. It seemed right to me. But Mum went all funny about it. We had a stupid argument, and then she said, 'You wear what you like then, but I'm going to wear my red coat whatever you say. Ben liked the fur on the collar. He used to stroke it.' And then she cried, and I realized I was being tactless and interfering so I shut up. I thought of offering to lend her my red scarf to go with it, just to show her that I was sorry, but something told me that it wouldn't be a good idea.

The church was full of flowers. It was strangely beautiful, like at a wedding. There were quite a lot of people there, some old friends of Mum's and Dad's and people who lived in our street. Mrs Russell was as near the front as she could get without sitting in the seats reserved for the family. She honestly looked as if she was enjoying herself.

Mr Henderson seemed different when he came in. Sort of solemn, but powerful and in command too. I felt at last that here was someone who understood what was going on. It was like being in a strange new building, and finding someone who's got the keys. Mr Henderson has got keys. I don't mean to the church hall or anything, but keys to secrets about life that he knows how to unlock.

I don't remember everything that happened at the funeral. I just remember the little coffin, shining, bathed in sunlight, speckled in jewel-like colours from the stained glass window, heaped up with white and yellow flowers. And I remember that the words of the service rolled on majestically, like waves breaking on a beach, and I remember that I no longer wanted to curse, and shout 'Where were you, God, the night Ben died?' I felt that somewhere there was a meaning, and one day I would know what it was, and that I was loved, and I had to trust that love, and let Ben go away into its arms, and one day I would go out into it too.

At the end of the service there was a silence, and then the vicar looked round us all, and he smiled, and said with a kind of power and confidence in his voice,

' "Blessed are the pure in heart, for they shall see God".'

I could tell it was a quote from somewhere. The Bible, I suppose. But it described Ben exactly. Pure in heart, that was Ben. It made Mum start crying again, and she clutched Dad's arm, but I found myself nodding, and Katy looked up at me, and she smiled, and I know she felt like I did, that Ben was safe with God.

Chapter Twelve

I can't remember much about the weeks after Ben's funeral. I suppose, being November, that it was wet, cold and gloomy. But I didn't seem to notice the weather, or anything else happening outside myself either. I had this dull, heavy pain, that sat on my chest like a weight, and nothing else mattered.

The strange thing was that life seemed to go on quite normally at school. I didn't know how to explain to anyone that to me things had changed completely, and changed for ever. I felt different from all the others, as if I was speaking a new language, or seeing through different glasses, or as if I'd gone into another dimension of life or something.

After a couple of weeks everyone at school seemed to think that it was all over, and that I must have got over Ben by this time, and they stopped being embarrassed or specially nice, or anything. In a way, that was a help. I had to go back to doing the same old things, like playing hockey, and getting

French homework in on time, and worrying about my low marks in Maths. But all the time, while I was pretending to be just the same as everyone else, I carried this churned up, desperate misery inside me.

Sometimes it lifted for a few moments. Occasionally, when I woke up in the morning, I felt quite ordinary again, and I'd think, 'That's nice. I haven't felt like this for ages. Why not?' and then I'd remember, and it would be as if the ton of concrete that was pressing down on my chest had got even heavier. Even in the daytime I had moments when I forgot about Ben. I'd be reading *Pride and Prejudice*, or having an argument about abortion or something, and then I'd suddenly realize I hadn't thought about him for half an hour.

At first, when that happened, I felt guilty, as if I'd betrayed him, and I'd whisper to myself,

'I'm sorry. I haven't forgotten. I'll never forget.' But then, slowly, the times when I wasn't thinking about him got longer, and the times when I was got shorter. And when I did think about him it got harder and harder to remember what he was really like, or to conjure up the sound of his voice, or the smell of his freshly washed hair.

At least things were better at home. Dad had

started his new job now. He had to leave the house early every day, and he got home quite late, but the main thing was that he didn't have to keep going away all the time. And Mum had stopped sniping at him, too. In fact, they'd got so lovey-dovey again all of a sudden that there didn't seem much room for anyone else.

Don't get me wrong. I hadn't exactly liked them going off each other. I mean, the last thing I wanted was a broken home, on top of everything else. It was just that they seemed as if they didn't need anyone except each other. When Dad was away, Mum had got into the habit of talking to me a bit about how she felt about things, but she didn't do it any more. Maybe she thought it would just make me feel worse, or something. Even when I knew she was miserable, she'd put on a show, and pretend to cheer up when I was around. It was only with Dad that she let her hair down, and he was the same with her. Nobody seemed to need me, not even Katy, much. Anyway, Katy doesn't really count as a person when it comes to that sort of thing. She's just a child.

People outside the family were just as bad. When anyone came to the house, they always seemed to think it was worst for Mum. And I suppose it was, in a way, but nobody seemed to think it was particularly sad for me. Maybe sisters don't usually love brothers the way I loved Ben. Maybe.

Not that many people came to the house after the first week or two. Mr Henderson called a few times, and some people came from the day centre Ben had started going to. But Mrs Russell was still in and out all the time, even though we were all fed up with her. Only two days after the funeral she marched in through the back door into the kitchen, and said to Mum, 'What are you going to do with all his things then, his clothes, and his cot and that?'

Mum went red and spoke quite sharply, 'We'll be making arrangements, thank you.'

And Mrs Russell said, 'Only there's my Sharon, and she's expecting her third after Christmas, and I know she could do with some new stuff, cheap.'

I sat there with my hands clenched, hoping that Mrs Russell would drop dead, or that lightning would strike the house, or that anything would happen to stop Mum giving Ben's precious things to Mrs Russell's nasty Sharon and Sharon's nasty babies, who always have runny noses and look spoilt and whiney. But I needn't have worried.

'I'll let you know if there's anything suitable,'

Mum said, and pressed her lips closely together so I could see she was annoyed. But after that, every time I saw Mrs Russell, I thought of her trying to get her hands on Ben's things and it made me boil. I didn't want anyone to touch them. They were sacred.

I hadn't been in Ben's room much since the funeral. I suppose Mum went in to clean as usual, because there was never any dust or anything in there. I don't know why, but I just didn't feel like going in. I didn't want to. I didn't even like it if the door was left open, so that I could see in when I went past to my own room. The empty cot, and the mobile hanging from the light, and the soft toys lined up on the chest of drawers gave me a sort of painful jolt, and I couldn't help thinking of the clothes in the drawers, still neatly folded up, ready to be used, just as they had been the day he died. The room had that sad, packaged up feel about it, like when people are just about to move away.

It was the moth that got things moving. I heard Dad swatting it on the stairs.

'That's the second this week,' he said, coming into the sitting room where I was supposed to be doing my homework and Mum was drying Katy's hair. 'They'll be into everything if we don't watch out. You should have seen Bill's father's coat when the moths got at it after it had been put away in a cupboard for six months.'

'What do you mean?' said Katy, looking alarmed. 'Do you mean they eat clothes? What about my new disco pants?'

That's typical Katy. Obsessed with clothes. I can't think where she gets it from. Mum's not a bit like that, and neither am I.

'Don't be silly,' said Mum, sort of absent-mindedly. 'Nobody's going to eat your disco pants. They only go for stuff that's not often used,' and I saw that she was looking steadily at Dad.

'We'll have to go through it all sometime, love,' said Dad gently. 'It can't just sit there for ever. I think the moment's come, don't you?'

Mum stood perfectly still, the hairbrush raised in one hand, the hairdryer in the other, poised over Katy's head.

'Ow!' said Katy, twisting round as the heat got too much for her scalp.

Mum pushed the hairdryer and the brush into my hands.

'You finish her off, Anna,' she said, and she followed Dad out of the room and up the stairs.

It was too much. It was like all the other things they'd done over the past few weeks. They were pushing me out. Shutting me off, as usual. Treating me as if I didn't exist. I flung the brush down and thrust the hairdryer at Katy.

'You can do your own hair for a change,' I said, 'and your eyebrows too if you like,' and I stormed off up the stairs to Ben's room, and threw the door open.

'What about me?' I burst out. 'It's my business just as much as yours. Why can't I . . .?' and then I saw Mum and shut up. She was sitting on the floor, holding up the green dungarees Ben had worn all last summer, and tears were running down her cheeks.

'Do you remember,' she said, looking at Dad, 'the day we went to the funfair, and some idiot gave him candyfloss?'

'What are you doing with them?' I said, not feeling angry any more, but hurt instead. 'Why can't I help too?'

'You can,' said Dad. 'Sit down.'

It sounds daft to say this, but we were happy that evening, in a funny sort of way. It was almost a relief to take out the little vests and jackets and sleeping suits, and touch them again. They'd been lurking all these weeks like work that you know you've got to do, but you can't get round to doing it. Unfinished business. It was painful, but nice too, like touching a scar when it hasn't completely healed.

We sorted everything into piles, and we kept stopping to remember. Sometimes, we even laughed, in a watery sort of way. Sometimes we cried a bit. At least, Mum did, especially when she found the hat she'd made for Ben to wear. It was so big, and looked so strange and un-babyish beside all the other, normal baby clothes.

'He only wore it once,' she said, and she put it to one side, by itself.

'What are we going to do with them all then?' I said, when the drawers were empty. I suddenly realized that we couldn't just put them back in the cupboard and leave them there.

'Not the dustbin,' said Mum, firmly.

'Not Sharon, either,' I said, just as firmly.

'I think,' said Dad, looking at Mum with a sort of watchful expression on his face as if he thought she might explode or something, 'that we ought to take them down to the Oxfam shop.'

I opened my mouth to say 'No,' but then I shut it again. I saw a sudden picture in my mind's eye of a little ragged kid with one of those big pot bellies, holding out his hand for one of Ben's nice fluffy things to put on, and I liked it.

'Can't we just keep one or two?' I said, and Dad looked relieved.

'Good idea,' he said, but he was still looking at Mum.

She reached out without a word, and pulled a couple of things out of the piles – a little red cardigan, and a pair of furry slippers, and an embroidered bib. But when Dad looked at me, and waited for me to take something, I found I couldn't. I couldn't bear to touch the clothes again. They were cold and lifeless. I suddenly wanted them to go, to be out of the house.

'It's all right,' I said, 'I can always look at Mum's pile if I want to,' and I got up and left them to it. Dad had already started packing things into plastic bags, and I didn't feel like helping.

He must have taken them down to the Oxfam shop while I was at school the next day, because when I came home, Ben's room was empty. Even the cot had gone. There was just the old chest of drawers in there, and the spare bed, that someone had moved in from Katy's room.

Chapter Thirteen

Spring came at last. It was almost a surprise. I'd got to feeling that winter and the darkness and cold would last for ever. But when it came, it sort of came in my mind, too.

I was still working at Mrs Chapman's on Saturdays. It was great, actually. She wasn't like other people, who mostly shied away from the subject of Ben as if it was indecent to talk about him or something. She often mentioned him, in a casual, ordinary way, as if he was still alive. It made me feel better, I don't know why.

I'd got used to the work in the shop. I didn't have to think about it much any more. I knew where everything was, and I knew a lot of the customers, too. Quite often there were gaps when no one came in, even though Saturday morning was one of the busiest times of the week, and when I wasn't in the middle of dusting the shelves, or unpacking a new delivery of pencil sharpeners, I had time to daydream. Mrs Chapman laughed at me, and said my head was so high up in the air I'd never keep my feet on the ground, but she didn't mean to be nasty.

One morning, I was in a particularly dreamy mood. I'd seen a beautiful film on TV the night before, and it had filled me full of a sort of mellow yearning. A dark-haired woman was buying a newspaper up at the counter, waiting for Mrs Chapman to finish serving someone else and take her money. I went down to the front of the shop to re-stock the rack of newspapers that hung just outside the doorway. When I turned back, and went round the central island to check on the stationery, I was jerked out of my daydream.

A pushchair was parked right up next to the freezer, where the ice creams were kept. The little girl, sitting quietly in it, was disabled. She had round, plastic, National Health glasses on, which were barely held up by her small button nose. Her head was a slightly unusual shape, and her eyes had that Asiatic look, pulled up at the edges. Her tongue was sticking out a bit, and a line of dribble ran down her chin. It wasn't the little girl who gave me the shock, though. It was the position in which her mother had left the pushchair. It was exactly where

I had left Ben, that morning when Miranda had seen him for the first time. I'd chosen the spot because I'd thought it was out of sight. I knew for sure, I was absolutely certain, that this little girl's mother had left her here for exactly the same reason. Memories came flooding back. My heart turned over.

'Ben,' I thought. 'Oh, Ben.'

The little girl looked up at me. Most people wouldn't have called her pretty. They wouldn't have seen past the things that made her look different. But she looked lovely to me. The eyes behind her glasses were big, and fringed with long black lashes. Her hair, black and straight, was tied in two bunches on each side of her head, and it looked as soft as feathers. It was hard to tell her age. I guessed she was about four. She smiled when she saw me looking at her, and leaning forward in her pushchair, she flapped her hand in my direction and blew a big bubble out of her mouth. I heard footsteps coming down the shop, and sensed that her mother was behind me, waiting for me to finish whatever I was doing and go back to the counter. Instead, I knelt down by the pushchair, and tickled the little girl under her ear.

'You're nice, aren't you?' I said. 'What a beautiful smile you've got!'

She wriggled with pleasure, put one fat little hand over her mouth, then put it out towards me.

'Aren't you clever! You can blow kisses!' I said. 'I bet they're all in love with you at home.'

The woman behind me had made no move. I turned to look at her. She looked defensive, and wary. She was watching me carefully. She didn't know what I was up to. She almost looked too old to be the little girl's mother. Her strong, dark hair was streaked with grey. She looked too kind of elegant, too, to have a young kid. She had on the kind of coat my mum doesn't even dare look at in the shops, and she was wearing these really modern metal earrings. She smiled at me hurriedly, as though she wanted to get out of my way, squeezed past me to get behind the pushchair, and moved towards the door of the shop.

'What's your little girl's name?' I said. 'She's a darling, isn't she?'

The woman looked at me in surprise. I could guess she wasn't used to people telling her that. Then she gave me a beaming smile. Her face changed completely.

'Jackie,' she said, in a slightly foreign accent. 'Her name's Jackie.' She hesitated. 'She's not quite . . .

not quite right. She's got Down's Syndrome.' She rolled the r, but said the medical term easily. It was obvious she'd said them many times before.

'She's not as disabled as my brother was,' I said.

'Your brother?' she said enquiringly. I knew I had caught her interest now.

'Yes,' I said, 'I had a brother who was, well, very disabled. But he was . . .' to my embarrassment I heard my voice shaking. 'He was lovely,' I finished lamely.

She tactfully stopped looking at me, bent over Jackie, did up a button on her little coat, and caressed her cheek with the tips of her fingers. I didn't realize till afterwards that she hadn't asked the usual question. Being foreign, perhaps she hadn't noticed that 'was' in the past tense. Or perhaps she was just too tactful to ask.

'Goodbye,' she said. 'See you again, maybe.'

'I hope so,' I said. 'Goodbye Jackie. Be a good girl now,' and I went to the shop door to watch them as they scurried down the street, until they had turned into the butcher's and were lost to view.

I saw Jackie and her mother quite often after that. They obviously liked coming into Mrs Chapman's, like I used to with Ben. They felt her friendliness, and kindly interest, so different from the averted eyes up at the supermarket. Mrs Maynard (I learned her name because she put in an order for a foreign newspaper) didn't talk much at first. She wasn't a chatty kind of person. But Mrs Chapman soon got her going. Mrs Chapman would have coaxed a brick wall to talk to her if there'd been no one else around. You could tell Mrs Maynard was lonely. She'd only just moved to this neighbourhood, she said, and she was alone with Jackie most of the time. She never mentioned her husband, but she looked so mournful a lot of the time I sort of assumed she was a widow. I listened with half an ear while the two of them were talking, but the rest of me was busy with Jackie.

Every time they came, Jackie and I had our little chat. I remembered what Ben had liked, and I guessed she'd like it too. Mrs Maynard would push her up to the counter (she didn't hide her anymore) and I'd blow Jackie a kiss. She'd blow one back, then I'd kneel down, and point to her shoes, and say 'Nice shoes,' or something, and work slowly upwards, saying 'What pretty socks,' or 'What a lovely dress,' and things like that till I got to the ribbon in her hair. I must say, she was always beautifully turned out. Mrs Maynard adored her. You could see that. And she was cute, Jackie was. If I missed out something, she'd grab my hand, and make me touch it, so that I had to be sure to notice everything, in the right order. And when we'd finished our little pantomime, I'd give her something out of one of the big jars Mrs Chapman kept behind the counter, full of toffees, and peppermint creams, and boiled sweets wrapped in cellophane. Mrs Chapman didn't mind. She only said that I had to square it with Mrs Maynard first, because these days you never knew what kind of funny notions mothers might have about their child's diet.

'I can't see that a few sweets now and then could harm a kiddie,' she said. 'But then I'm old-fashioned.'

I said nothing. You only had to look at Mrs Chapman to see that she had a fondness for sweets herself, but I thought it was best to keep a tactful silence on any subject that was remotely connected with weight.

Jackie used to go wild with joy when she got her sweet. Lots of kids, when they get a treat, whine and whinge for another before they've even got the wrapping off the first. You see some nasty little brats when you work in a shop like Mrs Chapman's.

It makes you wonder sometimes. I always used to think Mum was much too strict but I'm glad now that she brought me up properly. There's nothing worse than a snivelling, spoiled child. Jackie wasn't a bit like that. She knew the art of enjoying things in a simple, wholehearted way without having half an eye to anything else that might be forthcoming.

When they were ready to go, I'd nip down to the door of the shop, if there wasn't a queue waiting to be served, and wave bye-bye to Jackie. She couldn't say any words, except 'mumumum', which might have meant 'Mum', I suppose, but she knew how to wave bye-bye all right.

'God's little clowns, they call those kids,' said Mrs Chapman, heaving a sentimental sigh. 'You've got a lovely touch with her, Anna. Make a good mum yourself one day.'

I was sick of people saying things like that to me. Mrs Chapman was like Mum. She said it because she thought it would encourage me, but it had the opposite effect. It reminded me of how I used to feel – that I was a flop, a failure, a nit-wit, a Pea-brain, and that no boy had ever even sent me a Valentine card (except one from Joe once, because Miranda had put him up to it, but that didn't count), let alone asked me out.

I'd given up all hope of seeing Tony again. He'd been a shadowy dream figure for so long that he was little more than a name and an impression to me now. I'd almost forgotten what he looked like. I'd sort of forgotten about Jeff, too. I don't know why, but after Ben died I hadn't gone to the youth club. I hadn't really meant to give it up, but I'd missed a couple of weeks, and then another, and then it seemed sort of embarrassing to go again. But in the back of my mind I had a feeling that sometime I'd go back, only next time I wouldn't be all shy and awkward. I'd be confident and relaxed.

On the outside, I suppose I was the same, but inside I knew I was changing. I wasn't the same twit who could be knocked out cold for six months just by seeing a boy at the tennis courts. I suppose, once you've thought so much about death, you feel you've got a stronger hold on life, in a funny sort of way. You feel more daring, and that your time is precious. You don't want to waste it worrying about not being as good as everyone else. And that makes you look at other people more clearly too. Like I said, I felt as if I was seeing the world through a new kind of glasses.

Mrs Maynard didn't come in the next Saturday. At lunchtime I said to Mrs Chapman, 'No Jackie today, then?'

'No,' she said. 'They came in yesterday, though. Had a card to put in my window. She's looking for someone to look after Jackie for three weeks in the summer. Come to think of it, Anna, why don't you take her phone number? It would be just the job for you.'

As soon as she said it I knew she was right. Dad had booked up a holiday this year, but that would only be for two weeks at the end of the summer, and I'd given up the idea of tennis coaching. I was getting sick of being taught all day long. I fancied being in charge of someone else for a change. Looking after Jackie, I could earn some money and enjoy myself at the same time.

Suddenly, I felt I had to get the job. And the card in the window was a threat. Supposing someone else had spotted it and phoned up Mrs Maynard already? I watched in agonies as a young mum with a toddler stopped outside and read through all the adverts on the window. I willed the one about Jackie to drop off and disappear, but it didn't. If anything, it seemed to get bigger.

It was practically luminous in my eyes. I saw the woman open her bag, take out a pencil and start writing something down. I couldn't bear it any longer.

'Please, Mrs Chapman,' I said, 'can I phone Mrs Maynard now? I'm scared someone else'll get there first.'

She laughed.

'Cat on hot bricks you've been the last ten minutes,' she said. 'So that's the problem, is it? Yes, go ahead my love. I don't mind. Phone's still out the back if it hasn't walked.'

I knew as soon as Mrs Maynard picked up the receiver that I'd be all right. I'm often like that about phone calls. It must be my psychic sense again. At first though, it seemed as if I'd got it wrong. She sounded rather stiff.

'Yes? What do you want?' she said, and her foreign accent sounded more obvious than ever over the phone.

'It's about your advert in the newsagent's,' I said, suddenly breathless with nerves.

'Yes?' she said, sounding even more guarded.

'It's me,' I said stupidly. 'You know me. I'm Anna. I'm the girl who works for Mrs Chapman in

the shop on Saturdays. I know Jackie. I often talk to
her. You . . .'

She interrupted me. It was as if a cork had come
out of a bottle. I had to hold the phone six inches away
from my head like Mum does with Aunty Janice. It
took me a while to untangle what she said, but the
gist of it was that yes, she knew who I was, and yes,
I was just the right person, and would I really do it,
and she'd pay me properly, and I wouldn't believe
how worried she'd been about leaving Jackie with a
stranger, and she'd had a couple of funny calls after
she'd put up her advert, and she'd got so nervous
(only she pronounced it 'nerrr-vous') she'd nearly
decided not to go on this course after all, but she
wanted to so badly because she'd been on her own
with Jackie for four years, because her husband
had left her after Jackie was born, and she'd have
to get back to work in the end, wouldn't she, and
didn't I agree that the right way to start was to go
on a refresher course, because she'd been a bilingual
secretary, Italian and English, but she'd never used
computers and these days didn't I think it was
pointless even to try for a job unless you did?

All I had to do was stand there and say,
'Yes, no, yes, no,' and worry about Mrs

Chapman's phone bill, but at long last she paused to breathe, and I asked when did she want me to start. That set her off again. Only now she went on about Jackie, and how affectionate she was, and how nice it was to have such a loving child, and how important it was to be patient and slow, and how I'd be the right person because I had such a heart, because of my brother, and how safe she would feel with Jackie in such good hands.

I saw an opening then, and quickly said that Mrs Chapman was waiting for me, and she yelled her address at me two or three times, and I said I'd be in touch nearer the time.

'Told her your life story then, did you?' said Mrs Chapman drily, when I got back into the shop at last. I could see she was put out with me for being on the phone for so long. She's funny about the phone. She never uses it unless she has to, and when she does she talks in a loud, high-pitched voice, in short sharp sentences, as if she was using a code or something. But I'd been well trained by Dad. He's neurotic about the phone bill too. So I fished out two pounds and put it in the till.

'You don't have to do that, love,' said Mrs Chapman, but I could tell she was mollified. And she didn't take it out again either.

It wasn't until I got home that evening and was sitting in front of the telly that I realized how excited I was. Dad was lovely about it.

'Earning your own living already,' he said. 'I'll be nice to you now, Pollyanna, so you'll buy me a Porsche when you've made your first million.'

Katy was jealous.

'Oh, you are lucky,' she said. 'It's not fair. You'll have lots more money than me, and you don't even like buying clothes.'

Mum was guarded.

'It's a good idea,' she said. 'I'm sure you'll be a great help to Mrs Maynard, but you'll have to be a bit less scatty in someone else's house. The mess in your bedroom . . . !'

But they'd all got it wrong. It wasn't the money I was after. It wasn't even the feeling of being out at work. I just wanted to be with a child again. A special child who would need me. A child like Ben.

Chapter Fourteen

That night, I had a strange dream. I was sunbathing in a big park, near a lake, and there were lots of people out enjoying themselves. And all of a sudden a little hand caught at my leg, and I sat up. It was Ben.

He looked up at me, and laughed and laughed, putting his head on one side in the adorable way he had. And I said, 'Ben! Where have you been? Why did you leave us? Who's looking after you? Are you all right?'

Then Mrs Maynard came up and said, 'He came to me, you know, and he's quite happy. I didn't like to tell you. They wouldn't let me. They had reasons, I'm sure.'

And then Ben rolled away very fast, towards the lake, and I ran after him, but the more I tried the slower I got, and when I did reach him he was slippery, as if his body was covered with oil, and I couldn't pick him up. He slithered into the water, and sank, and I saw his face lying quite still, with

ripples above gently distorting it. It was his dead
face, that I'd seen in his coffin.

I tried and tried to plunge in and get him out, but
Mrs Maynard stopped me, and we fought on the edge
of the lake. My arms and legs were caught, held in
her vice-like grip. And then she let me go, and said,
'Look.'

I looked down into the water, and Ben's eyes
were open, and he was smiling at me, and it was his
living face again. And he turned over like a little fish,
so free and happy, without any of the awkwardness
or jerkiness he'd had in real life, supple and strong,
and he swam away, into the middle of the lake, and
disappeared. I burst out crying, and kept calling
and calling to him to come back, but Mrs Maynard
turned me round, and there was Jackie, grizzling in
her pushchair. Mrs Maynard said, 'She's seen a little
girl over there with an ice cream. Can you get her
one, Anna?'

I woke up then, hot and sweating, and all tangled
up in my sheet which had wound itself round my
legs. I lay there for a long time, savouring the
closeness to Ben, looking with my mind's eye at his
face as it appeared in the dream. I'd often tried to
remember what he looked like, but I could only see

him as he appeared in photographs. In my dream he'd been absolutely real, himself, so close to me, but so horribly out of reach. I cried in earnest then, and it was as if he'd just died, the grief was so new. It twisted me all up inside, and I felt it would always be there, as fresh and as agonizing as on the day he was buried.

The funny thing was, though, that by the time I'd got up and had breakfast, the living image of Ben had faded again, and when Mum asked me what I was intending to take on holiday, and would I like a new bathing costume because she'd seen some down the high street, I was nearly back to normal all of a sudden. It was as if a crack in a wall had appeared, and I'd been able to peep into another room, but the crack had been plastered over again, and there was no way I could open it up.

I'd told Mrs Maynard that we'd be going away in the middle of August, and she fixed to go on her course at the beginning of the holidays, so it was soon after the end of term that I found myself on the doorstep of the flats where she lived, ringing the front bell and waiting for the door buzzer to sound.

It's always a funny feeling, going into someone's place for the first time. You see things so sharply. It's like I said, first impressions are the important ones. Mrs Maynard's flat was small but it was very neat and tidy. There were no odd chairs and cushions in random, dingy colours like there are in our house. There were no drooping, straggling houseplants that everyone forgets to water, or shelves piled untidily with odd bits and pieces. There wasn't any mess. Everything had been neatly put away. One day, I thought, when I had my own place, it would be like this, all neat and tidy, and properly looked after, and uncluttered.

The best thing was that Jackie was so pleased to see me. She ran straight up to me, put her arms round my leg, and rested her head against my knee. It was the first time I'd seen her since my dream, and I felt quite choked up for a moment. I bent down and picked her up, and she hugged me, and patted my hair. Then she struggled to be free, so I put her down and she tugged at my hand.

'She wants to show you her chair in the kitchen,' said Mrs Maynard, with the indulgent voice she always used when she talked about Jackie. 'Go with her. We'll show you round the whole flat so you'll know where to find everything.'

The tour didn't take long. There was the kitchen,

the small living room with a shelf of toys all standing in a tidy line, the bathroom and Jackie's room. She didn't show me her own bedroom properly, though I was dying to see it. She just opened the door a crack, giving me a glimpse of a peach coloured bedspread, and passed on. The last door she didn't open at all.

'This is my son's,' she said. 'He's away at college. I don't know if he comes this week. With boys you never know!'

It was hours before Mrs Maynard had finished giving me my instructions. Jackie had to have her routine, she said. She liked to have her snack at eleven, then her walk to the shops or the park, where she was allowed to play in the sandpit but not go down the slide. Didn't I agree that it was too dangerous? And she could not go into the playground at all if there were a lot of rough children there who might push her over. Then she had to come home by half past twelve and have her lunch. Mrs Maynard would leave it every day in a special place in the fridge and all I had to do was take it out and heat it up. She had to eat it with her own spoon, and then I would sing her some nursery rhymes, and she would have a nap, and then we should play together, and I had to make sure that she didn't touch any electric plugs, or fall off the sofa, or get too cold. Then at four o'clock it would be time for her milk and biscuits, and soon after that Mrs Maynard should be home. Had I understood everything? Would I like her to run through it all over again? She had written some notes for me on this piece of paper. Perhaps they would be enough.

At long last she picked up her bag and actually got herself out of the front door. But I wasn't at all surprised to hear the key in the lock two minutes later.

'The potty! I forgot about the potty!' she said, and then she had to show me where it was kept, neatly tucked under the washbasin in the bathroom, and explain the sign Jackie used when she needed it.

At last she had gone.

For a few minutes I did nothing. I just sat there, enjoying the peace, and the lovely feeling of being in charge. It made me think all over again of that red dawn when Ben was born. Then a clock chimed somewhere, and I jumped to my feet. It was eleven o'clock already. Time for Jackie's snack. I couldn't afford to let the routine slip only five minutes into Day One.

I'd been all nervy before I started the job in case

I'd gone rusty on looking after a child, but after that first day, when I seemed to be running in circles to keep to Mrs Maynard's precious routine, and was worried anyway about doing everything right and remembering all the instructions, I found I slipped into it as easy as winking. There was no point, of course, in pretending that Jackie was Ben. She wasn't. She never would be. She could never begin to take his place. Even so, although I told myself all the time that she wasn't the same, I still kept on falling into the trap of expecting her to do the same kinds of things. But in every way, Jackie was miles ahead of Ben. She could walk, for one thing, and use the potty (though she forgot it sometimes), and ask for what she wanted by pointing to it, though she couldn't say a word. She could do other clever things too, like singing along with me in a wordless hum when I sang to her.

It didn't take me long to realize that Jackie had been spoiled, and wrapped in cotton wool since the day she was born. Mrs Maynard was so frightened that she might do herself an injury, that Jackie had never been allowed to do anything by herself. She wouldn't try to go up and down stairs by herself, or climb on to a chair, or turn on a tap. She'd stand at

the top of the steps going down to the street from
the flat, and wait patiently till I was ready, then she'd
put out her arms and expect to be carried down. No
wonder Mrs Maynard looked exhausted so much of
the time. Jackie was small for a four-year-old, but
she was still a tidy weight. I realized too that Mrs
Maynard was in the habit of waiting on Jackie hand
and foot. She hadn't even tried to teach her to put
her own socks on, or to wash her own hands.

It was realizing that which made me ambitious.
Jackie, I was sure, was capable of much more than
Mrs Maynard realized. I began to think out a plan of
all the things I could teach her. I wouldn't tell Mrs
Maynard. I'd surprise her when Jackie had learned
something really spectacular, like brushing her own
hair.

Mind you, I began to regret after a while that I'd
started on hair. On my first two days, Jackie had
stood quite still, as good as a doll, waiting for me to
do it for her. But after that I didn't let her get away
with it. She had to join in the whole operation with
me. The trouble was, I had no idea that hair was so
difficult. Ben had never got near being able to cope
with that kind of thing, so it was all new ground for
me. I began to see how many different things you do

when you do your hair, like holding the brush so that the bristles are pointing down, and then pulling it in the right direction. And when you've done one side, you've got to start all over again on the other side without messing up the bit you've done. Incredibly complicated. Think it out sometime. You'll see what I mean.

I tried first just showing Jackie how I did my own hair. That didn't take me very far. She couldn't concentrate for more than a couple of seconds at a time. Then I put the brush in her hand, and sort of stroked her head.

'Jackie do it,' I said. She smiled at me, her little pink tongue as ever poking out from between her teeth, but without the faintest sign of comprehension.

'Jackie do her own hair,' I said again, and dropping on my knees in front of her, I put the brush into her hand, and curled her fingers round it. Then together, we pulled it through her hair. She roared with laughter. This was a lovely new game. But she had no idea what I was getting at.

'Look,' I said, and I did it again. 'Now Jackie do it.'

After five minutes I thought we'd done enough for one day. Anyway, I was getting bored and so was

Jackie. I dressed her, carried her downstairs, found the pushchair, strapped her in it, and went off to the shops. I was dying to show her off to Mrs Chapman.

I was so busy steering the pushchair and worrying about Jackie dropping her teddy on the pavement (Mrs Maynard had very strict views on hygiene) that I almost walked straight past Debbie without seeing her. She came up behind me and touched my arm.

'So this is your famous holiday job is it?' she said, looking at Jackie. She sounded sarcastic. I had obviously caught her on a bad day.

'Yes, this is Jackie,' I said, looking down with pride, and checking quickly that her nose didn't need a wipe. 'Isn't she gorgeous?'

'Matter of taste I suppose,' said Debbie.

I looked up, shocked. I'd forgotten how awful Debbie could be. She'd been so nice to me over Ben that I'd got sort of lulled into a false sense of security. But perhaps I was tougher now than I'd been a couple of years ago, or perhaps I'd just learned a thing or two from Katy. Anyway, I stopped myself from rushing full-tilt to Jackie's defence, and said,

'How's your job going then?'

'I haven't got one,' said Debbie flatly. She didn't say any more, but I knew, because Miranda had told me, that she tried, and failed, to get taken on by a couple of boutiques. It was the only kind of holiday job she'd consider doing, she'd been heard to say grandly, because most other kinds of temporary work were so demeaning.

'Serves you right for being so choosy,' I wanted to say, and was surprised at myself. I hadn't ever thought of criticising Debbie before. She went on down the road, and I looked after her, wondering for the millionth time how she managed to walk without the slightest bottom wiggle at all, when a thought suddenly struck me. Debbie was still just as beautiful, of course, but in a kind of way that I could see, for the first time, wasn't very attractive. When you looked at her you could tell that she'd spent hours ironing out every last crease on her blouse, and more hours still scraping every last hair off her legs, but the result was almost too perfect. It made her seem cold. Miranda didn't have a straight nose, or wonderful hair, or huge eyes, and she looked a crumpled mess most of the time, but she had warmth and sexiness dripping off the ends of her fingers.

'Poor old Debbie,' I suddenly thought, as I realized that in spite of all her airs and graces she'd never had a proper boyfriend.

As usual I talked to Mrs Chapman about it when Jackie and I finally got to her shop, after an expensive and time-consuming ten minutes at the ice cream van, which I knew Mrs Maynard wouldn't approve of. Mrs Chapman wasn't a gossip, because she never passed tit-bits on, but she'd got this kind of thirst to hear about other people's lives. It was how she built up her phenomenal knowledge of human nature, I suppose.

'I knew someone like your Debbie once,' she said. 'Skin like eggshell she had, and lovely long white hands. She was so pretty she'd have made a beautiful calendar, hanging on the wall there. Funny thing was, though, she never got married. Boys used to turn round, and whistle and all that, but give them five minutes of her high and mighty talk and they'd be off. She went on being beautiful till she was a poor old girl like me. Had a passion for cats. Looked lovely, they did, curled up on her lap. Seems a shame, though, doesn't it? A waste of all them good looks, if you ask me.'

I thought about Debbie on and off for the rest of the day. It was as if a spell had been broken. I'd been grovelling all these years, never sticking up for myself, always feeling grateful for the slightest crumbs of attention, and here I was free at last, not caring any more whether she was nice to me or not.

'There's more to friendship than that,' I thought, and way down at the bottom of my mind was an irritating whisper which I tried to smother.

'Perhaps Mum was right about her after all. She does need her bottom smacked.'

I didn't tell Mrs Maynard about the progress we were making with the hair. For one thing, I wanted to give her a surprise. For another, we were going so slowly. Every day I spent longer and longer at it, guiding Jackie's fingers, showing her, talking, encouraging, until in the end she really began to cotton on. And once she'd started she got the idea quicker than I'd ever expected. One minute she was standing there, breathing heavily, fingers working cumbersomely, tongue sticking out further and further, and the next minute she'd made a proper stroke, and then another, and then another. She'd done it!

She knew at once that she'd been a clever girl. She clapped, and laughed, and wriggled with pleasure. I was so pleased I picked her up and danced about with her in my arms.

'Clever Jackie! Brilliant Jackie! Clever little girl!'

I sang to her. I was making so much noise I didn't hear the front door open and shut, and when I did hear someone come into the room behind me I'd got my hair all tangled up in the buckle on Jackie's dungarees and couldn't look up. I couldn't wait, though, to tell Mrs Maynard the news.

'You'll never guess what,' I said, busy with my hair, 'clever Jackie's learned to brush her hair all by herself, haven't you, my love?'

There was no answer. I got myself untangled, and turned to look at Mrs Maynard. But it wasn't Mrs Maynard.

In the doorway stood Tony.

Chapter Fifteen

It's one thing to decide, very sensibly, that the person you've been dreaming about for the last year doesn't matter to you any more, and anyway that you'd rather have someone funny and kind, with bubbly fair hair and an ordinary face. But when you turn round unexpectedly, and your daydream is actually standing there, right in front of you, and electric flashes are going off like fireworks, it's another matter, I can tell you. In spite of myself I felt my heart pounding, and it seemed as if an egg beater had got into my stomach.

I'd imagined Tony so much, I suppose I'd built up a false picture in my mind. The real person was shorter, or maybe I'd grown. And although he was good-looking, and pantherish, and all those other things, he didn't have that kind of shining, heroic glow I'd seen round him that first time.

He came into the room, and looked at me, frowning.

'Where's my mother?' he said. 'Who are you?'

'Mrs Maynard's out,' I said. My voice started on a kind of squeak, and I had to cough to cover it up. 'I'm here to look after Jackie.'

His beautiful black eyebrows plunged down to his nose as he frowned.

'Mother's *out?*' he said. 'She never goes out. She's never been known to leave Jacqueline for more than thirty seconds at a time since the day she was born.'

'She's doing a course,' I said, only able to produce short sentences owing to the tight band that was tied round my chest and was stopping me breathing. 'Computing. She wants to go back to work.'

'Well well.' He dropped the smart leather bag he was carrying and came into the room. Then he looked at me again. The crossness left his face, and the charm suddenly returned. It made me feel weak at the knees.

'Haven't I seen you before?' he said.

'Yes,' I said, 'last summer at the tennis courts.'

He screwed up his face and thought.

'Joe and Barny,' he said at last, 'and that awful girl who giggles all the time and bites her fingernails.'

'Miranda,' I said, giggling a bit to myself to think of the hours of wasted passion that Miranda had lavished on the memory of Tony.

He moved into the kitchen, stepping over a pile of toys with which Jackie was quietly playing. He didn't look at her, or greet her or anything, and I suddenly realized that Jackie hadn't exactly rushed up to him either. It was odd for her. She usually flung herself at anyone who came to the flat. The milkman and the postman adored her. They always turned to wave as they went down the street, and she would stand at the window till they were out of sight.

I heard the clink of glasses in the kitchen.

'Hey!' Tony called. 'What's your name?'

'Anna.'

'Have a drink, Anna. Wine?'

I was terribly embarrassed. For a start I didn't drink usually, and certainly not in the middle of the afternoon. And then I felt it would be all wrong to drink on the job. What if Mrs Maynard suddenly came home and found me with a glass in my hand? She'd probably give me the sack on the spot. But on the other hand, it seemed silly and childish to refuse.

'Not now, thanks,' I mumbled, sounding weak even to myself.

'Go on,' he said. 'Why not? It'll do you good.'

He came back into the sitting room with a glass in

each hand. I took mine and sipped it. Then I put it
down behind a pot plant and hoped Tony wouldn't
notice. He didn't. He was obviously not a very
noticing kind of person. He sat down on the sofa,
crossed his legs, and stretched one arm out along the
back.

'How did you meet my mother?' he said.

Perhaps it was the way he said the word 'mother',
or perhaps it was something in his face, or perhaps
it was my famous sixth sense which told me that he
and Mrs Maynard didn't hit it off too well.

'I've got a Saturday job in a shop,' I said, pleased
to find that my voice was under control at last.
'Your mother advertised there for a babysitter, and
I answered the advert. I've often seen her coming in
with Jackie, and Jackie and I got to be friends.'

I looked over quickly to make sure Jackie was
all right. She had put something in her mouth.
I went over and fished it out. It was a paper clip.
Mrs Maynard would have had a fit. I looked round,
found the box she'd taken it out of, and moved it to
a higher shelf. According to the timetable, I should
have been playing with her at the moment, but she
seemed quite happy on her own. Anyway, I couldn't
possibly concentrate on playing with Jackie since

Tony had arrived. I was beginning to relax a bit. My heart was just about beating normally again. The only funny symptom now was a feeling of intense awareness. Everything looked brighter than usual.

I dared to ask a question.

'Are you staying long?'

He laughed.

'What? Here? Not likely. I'm off next week to stay with my Dad. He's got a fabulous house in France, and I get to drive around in the Ferrari. Who'd stay here?'

I didn't say anything, but he must have sensed that I was dying to ask a million questions. He shrugged and spread out his hands. He talked perfect English, but he sometimes used a kind of foreign gesture which made him seem exotic and cosmopolitan.

'Look,' he said. 'If you want to know about the Maynard family, I'll tell you. My father's English and my mother's Italian. They split up four years ago, and my father's company sent him to France. He makes a lot more money over there than he ever could in this God-awful country. My mother devotes herself all the time to Jacqueline,' (I wondered again why he didn't call her by her nickname) 'and I am in the middle of a brilliant university career.'

He laughed to show that he was teasing, and
tossed his head back to flick the long mane of hair
out of his eyes. The movement made me look away,
and I caught sight of the clock. It was nearly four,
and Jackie hadn't had her milk and biscuits! Mrs
Maynard would be back any minute, and she'd find
me neglecting my duties in the middle of a drunken
orgy with her son!

I leapt to my feet. I'd taken off my shoes and curled
up in a big armchair while we were talking, and in
getting up I kicked them right under the sideboard.
I had to get down on my hands and knees to fish
them out. I was irritated with myself for being so
awkward, and looking such a ninny. Tony was so
sleek, and kind of elegant. I looked crumpled and
hot.

I picked up his empty wineglass, fetched out my
full one from behind its plant, but with my back
between it and Tony so that he couldn't see how
little I'd drunk, and carried them through to the
kitchen. Jackie followed me. I felt her arms go round
my leg and her head cuddle into the side of my jeans.
I reached down and picked her up.

'Let's take your cardigan off, shall we?' I said. I'd
forgotten how thrilled I'd been about the brushing.

It obviously wouldn't interest Tony, and suddenly it seemed much less important to me. Then I only had time to settle Jackie down with her milk, wash and dry the wine glasses and whisk the bottle out of sight when I heard Mrs Maynard's key in the lock, and her excited voice saying, 'Tony!' as she stepped into the sitting room.

I know you're not supposed to eavesdrop, but I couldn't help overhearing everything from the kitchen. Even if I'd shut the door, I could still have heard through it. I didn't think about it much at the time, but it was a peculiar conversation for a mother and son who hadn't seen each other for three months.

Mrs Maynard's voice sounded almost nervous, 'Are you well, Tony? Are you all right?' and he sounded bored: 'Yes, of course. I've got a pile of stuff here that needs washing.' He hadn't got off the sofa or anything to give her a hug and a kiss. He just went on sitting there, with his arm still stretched out along the back. Mum would have said, 'Fine, you know where the washing machine is,' but Mrs Maynard only said, 'Don't worry, darling. I'll wash it for you.'

'There's another one that needs his bottom smacked,' I thought, and I couldn't help smiling at the thought of Mrs Maynard putting Tony across her knee.

When I got to work the next morning, Mrs Maynard was looking harassed. She was hovering anxiously over Jackie, trying to keep her quiet.

'Tony's still asleep,' she whispered, with her finger on her lips. 'He hates being woken early.'

I was envious. I love sleeping in too, but after about half past eight no one bothers to be quiet in our house. If you want to sleep in you just have to manage as best you can. The thought of everyone tip-toeing around at half past ten was amazing.

When I went into the kitchen I could see why Mrs Maynard looked tired. She'd obviously been busy with the heap of freshly washed clothes that were folded up on the kitchen table.

'Would you like me to iron them?' I said. Her face brightened.

'Yes please,' she said, 'but only when Jackie is taking her nap. She mustn't be running around when the iron is on.'

In the end, it was my fault that Tony eventually got up. I was getting Jackie dressed for her daily walk. I was trying so hard to be quiet that I'd picked up the brush and done her hair before I thought about what

I was doing. Jackie was furious. She suddenly threw a tantrum and started screaming.

'Sshh!' I said helplessly, 'you'll wake Tony!'

His bedroom door opened, and he stood there, all tousled, in his pyjamas.

'What the hell's going on?' he said. 'Can't you keep her quiet?' Then he saw me.

'Oh, it's you,' he said. 'Where's my mother?'

'She's gone to the college,' I said.

He yawned, and then he smiled at me.

'You wouldn't get me some breakfast, would you?' he said. 'I'm starving.'

Two days earlier, if I'd imagined having the chance of getting Tony his breakfast, I'd have died of bliss. But now that it was actually happening, I wasn't interested. For a start, poor old Jackie was still crying, and she needed to be comforted, and to go out for her walk, and then, even worse, I didn't know how to use the elaborate coffee machine that Mrs Maynard had in her kitchen, and I hadn't seen any instant coffee around the place. Somehow I was sure that Tony wouldn't drink tea for breakfast. Tea's a lot wetter than coffee, if you see what I mean, and Tony was anything but wet.

But at the same time, I didn't like to say no. I mean,

I was being paid to look after Jackie, so I thought maybe Mrs Maynard would expect me to look after Tony, too, like she would herself. Anyway, it was too late to say anything, because Tony had disappeared into the bathroom. So I hastily unscrambled Jackie, who was always easy to pacify, and left her with a biscuit, while I rushed into the kitchen to put the kettle on and lay out a plate and a knife and some butter and marmalade on the table. It seemed a bit indecent to talk to Tony through the bathroom door, so I just left everything I could think of out on the table, and got back to Jackie. She'd made a fine old mess with her biscuit, but I decided I'd clear it up when we got home, and we set off at last, me feeling frazzled, and Jackie happily following the route we took every day, never bored, always ready to play the same old games of 'Boo!' and to smile at everyone she met. That was one thing I never got used to with Jackie. She didn't come as a shock to people in the way that Ben had done. She was obviously disabled, of course, but she looked appealing too, and she had such a winning smile that most people smiled back at her, or even stopped for a chat.

Tony didn't appear at lunchtime. But afterwards, when Jackie was having her nap and I was doing his blessed ironing, he sat on the kitchen table watching me, and chatted. He looked marvellous. His hair was all moussed into shape, so you could still see the marks of the comb in it, and his clothes were so perfect they could have gone straight into a magazine. He wore them very well too. He'd got his collar turned up at a sort of angle, and his sleeves were rolled back, to look casual, but it must have taken ages to get the look exactly right. For a moment, I wondered how long he'd spent in the bathroom. He certainly didn't throw his clothes on like I did. He had the same effect on me as Debbie always had. I was acutely conscious of dirt under my fingernails, and the scuffs on my shoes.

But I could tell he liked me. He liked talking to me, anyway, because he didn't move but stayed on, watching me work round the kitchen, hanging his things up to air, or filling the iron with water to make it steam. He talked a lot. He told me about his father's house in France with the swimming pool and the live-in maid, and about the yacht they were going to buy, and he went on for hours about his father's Ferrari, with its special kind of gears or something. I didn't believe half of it, actually, but I liked hearing him talk. It was sort of fantasy, but it was more than I'd ever seen or done, and it was certainly more interesting than ironing. And I enjoyed thinking of how mad with jealousy Miranda would be if she could see me now.

Peace didn't last for long, though. I was ironing a shirt, and like Mum had shown me, I started with the collar. Tony suddenly leaned forward and whisked it off the ironing board.

'Look,' he said, irritated, 'you've done it all wrong. Look at these creases down at the points. I wouldn't be seen dead with a collar ironed like that. This is how you do it.'

He took the iron out of my hand and, with infinite care, smoothed out all the tiny creases. I felt humiliated.

'Perhaps you'd better finish it off then,' I said, trying not to sound huffy but not succeeding.

He raised his eyebrows.

'Ironing's hardly a man's job, is it?' he said.

'My dad does it,' I said, knowing that I sounded feeble but knowing I was right.

'Oh he does, does he?' Tony's scorn was unmistakeable. I felt suddenly furiously angry. I wasn't being paid to do all Tony's ironing. I didn't mind doing it, but I did mind him taking it for granted that I should. And I minded being criticized very much indeed. Anyway, I was supposed to be looking after Jackie. It was time to get her on to the potty.

'I'll stop there, then,' I said. 'I've got to get Jackie up now.'

'Jackie, Jackie,' he said, mimicking my voice. 'That's all anyone round here thinks of. What on earth do you all see in her? She should have been put in a home as soon as she was born. She's the cause of all the trouble in this family. She broke up my parents' marriage. Mum couldn't think of anything but her. No wonder Dad got fed up and went off with someone more interesting. I'd have done the same. Everything was fine before Jackie came on the scene. She's smashed this family up. It's so unfair!'

I gaped at him, astonished. The smooth talking, grown-up good-looker had gone, and in his place was a child, a small, vain, spoilt child, who was hurt, and angry. I felt much older than him all of a sudden. And strangely enough, I liked this Tony more than the other one. He was just like Katy. I could understanding him resenting Jackie, if she'd broken up his family. After all, poor old Ben could have done the same to us. And Tony had never had a chance to get fond of Jackie. Mrs Maynard had squeezed him out. He'd never been encouraged to look after her, or do things for her, and share her, like I'd shared Ben. His dad didn't sound much good either, with his daft ideas about men not having anything to do with babies and not being supposed to do the ironing.

I wasn't surprised Tony was so jealous. He'd obviously been the centre of his mother's life till Jackie came along, and although Mrs Maynard tried so hard to please him when he came home, there was no doubt that it was Jackie who now reigned supreme. Mrs Maynard ran in circles round her and everyone else came a poor second.

Jealousy was something I could understand. Even though I didn't particularly want to be best friends with Debbie any more, I still couldn't think of her going off with Emma without a pang. Jealousy was the worst feeling in the world. Poor old Katy had suffered over Ben, too. The difference was, though, that deep down Katy had really loved Ben. Jealousy had sort of got in the way of her showing it, but it hadn't stopped her being sorry when he died and giving him her bambi. We talked about it sometimes.

In fact, Katy and I talked about a lot of things these days. She was turning into a real friend.

Maybe there was hope for Tony yet. Maybe he'd turn into a real friend too.

Chapter Sixteen

Tony was actually up when I arrived the next morning. He was drinking a cup of coffee at the table. It was littered with the remains of his breakfast. He never bothered to clear anything up. If I didn't get round to it, Mrs Maynard did it all when she got home. He looked so sulky, I nearly laughed out loud.

'Morning,' I said. 'What's the matter with you, then?' The direct method sometimes works with Katy when she's cross. She can't resist telling you exactly what the matter is. But it failed with Tony.

'Get knotted,' he said.

'OK,' I said, and started tying myself in knots, you know, putting my head under one arm, and twisting one leg round the other till I looked as if I was in some kind of weird yoga position. He was behaving childishly, so I would, too. It worked, anyway. He laughed, a bit grudgingly, but it was still a laugh.

I took another risk.

'You know what,' I said. 'I fancy some of that

lovely coffee. Why don't you make me some?'

He looked faintly surprised. He was obviously not used to being asked to do things, particularly in the kitchen. But he got up, meek as a lamb, and ran some hot water from the kettle into the coffee pot.

'You're a funny girl, Anna,' he said, looking at me over my shoulder. I felt my heart give a tiny lurch, as if I was on the slippery slope of love again, he looked so handsome. But then he noticed a blob of marmalade that had landed on his spotless trousers, and he was so fussy, sponging it off and inspecting the damage that it put me right again.

'I'm not funny,' I said.

'Yes, you are,' he said. 'I don't know anyone else like you.'

'You can't know many other people then,' I said, feeling vaguely offended.

'No, I don't.' He had obviously taken me more seriously than I'd intended. 'Don't be deceived by the glittering front I present to the world. I'm a loner.'

'Haven't you got heaps of friends?' I was surprised. 'I thought that at university . . .'

'No,' he said, sounding all bitter and cynical. 'No heaps of friends at university. No real friends at all in fact. And no bloody family, either. That's life, dear, innocent little Anna. You're on your own, girl. Who cares if you live or die?'

I could tell he was play-acting a bit. He was trying to sound dramatic. But he meant some of it too.

'Your mum cares,' I said. 'She'd do anything for you.'

'Used to, you mean.' He brought the coffee pot over and poured some out for me. It was stronger than I liked, but it smelled delicious. He still sounded angry, but he'd dropped the affectation. 'If Mum had cared, she'd have tried a bit harder to keep this family together. But she didn't lift a finger to stop Dad going. All she could think about was Jackie. What's Jackie got that I haven't got, I'd like to know? I mean, look at her!'

We both turned to where Jackie was playing. She had put her head down on a cushion and stuck her bottom in the air. She was turning her face from side to side, obviously enjoying the feel of the velvet on her cheeks. She looked so funny even Tony had to laugh.

'Oh, all right,' he said. 'I can see she's quite sweet sometimes.'

'The trouble is,' I said, feeling as if I'd suddenly

uncovered a vital truth, 'you don't really know her.'

'What do you mean?' He looked offended. 'How can you *know* a kid like that? She can't even talk.'

'No,' I said, 'but there are lots of other things she can do. She's a real personality. Your mum's spoiled her, that's the problem.'

He laughed.

'You don't have to tell me that,' he said feelingly.

I didn't say, 'She's spoiled you, too,' but I was tempted. Instead, I said, 'Jackie could learn to do much more for herself than she does now. Your mum does it all for her.'

'What do you mean?' Tony yawned. He was beginning to look bored. I could see he wanted to get back to talking about himself.

'Well, she ought to be learning things like dressing herself, and helping tidy up her toys. You wouldn't believe it, but I've taught her already to brush her own hair.'

'Big deal,' said Tony.

'Yes,' I said, almost choking on my last mouthful of coffee. 'It is a big deal. It's a huge deal. It's a gigantic deal. And she's done it.'

He was taken aback.

'OK, OK,' he said. 'Don't bite me.'

But I had to show him.

'Jackie!' I called out to her. 'Come here, love. Time for your walk. Bring your hairbrush.'

She trotted obediently into her room, fetched her brush and came to stand beside me, one hand on my knee, smiling up at me expectantly.

I touched her hair.

'Do your hair, Jackie,' I said. She giggled and then, frowning hard, dribbling horribly, she lifted the brush to her head and began her task.

Tony watched with impatience.

'She's doing it all wrong,' he said. He leaned forward to take the brush from her.

I pulled his arm back.

'No! Let her try. You can see what an effort she's making. Don't take it away from her.'

In the silence that followed I could hear the electric clock above the cooker blipping away the seconds, and Jackie breathing heavily through her snuffly nose. Tony and I were completely absorbed. I stole a look at him. His fingers were itching to help. His mouth twitched in response to each fumbling movement. Like me, he was willing her to do it.

She managed three wobbling strokes down the right side of her head, and three more down the left.

'Now the back,' I said.

It was the hardest bit of all. The brush wavered through the soft black hair, and then it was done. Jackie gave a crow of joy, threw back her head and clapped her hands with delight. I heard Tony let his breath out with a whoosh.

He turned to me. 'She did it!'

'Well go on, then,' I said. 'Tell her how clever she is. She'll understand.'

'Clever girl, Jackie,' said Tony awkwardly. I had a funny feeling that he'd never really said anything to her before. Jackie was delighted. She wriggled some more, and her tongue stuck out further than ever.

'Put your tongue in, Jackie.' If I told her that once a day I said it a thousand times. She tucked it back in at once.

'She really seems to know what you're saying.' Tony looked astonished.

'Of course she does,' I said. 'Some things, anyway. Don't try any Shakespeare on her, that's all.'

'I don't get it,' said Tony. 'She wasn't like this last time I was at home.'

'Well how long ago was that?' Tony didn't look thick, but he obviously wasn't all that brilliant.

'Three months, I suppose.'

'Well, there you are then. A lot happens to a four-year-old in three months.'

'What else are you going to teach her?' Tony sounded quite enthusiastic.

'I don't know,' I said. 'She's got an awful lot to learn. I thought perhaps I'd try to get her to put her own jacket on.'

Tony looked critically at the jacket.

'Too difficult,' he said. 'She'd never manage the sleeves. I think you should go for the sandals. They've only got that funny sticky stuff on the straps, you know, velcro, or whatever it's called. No buckles or anything. That'd be easier.'

'Why don't you teach her?' I said.

He drew back at that.

'I'm a man, like I said, not a nanny.'

'Silliest thing I ever heard,' I said, sounding even to myself like a nursery nurse. 'You're a brother, aren't you? You've got a sister, haven't you, and she's alive. You're so lucky, you've got no idea.'

I stopped. I could feel myself getting worked up. I knew my face was going red.

Tony was looking at me curiously.

'What do you mean?' he said.

'My brother died,' I blurted out. 'He was much

worse than Jackie. He couldn't even walk. But he learned to do a lot of things. And you've got Jackie, and you don't even notice her. I'd give anything in the world to have Ben back again. Anything.'

And then, I can't think how I came to be such a fool, but I burst into tears and dashed off to the bathroom. I was there for quite a long time getting control of myself again, and then washing my face to make it look less red and splodgy, and flushing the loo to give the impression that that was all I'd been doing. When I finally came out, I couldn't believe my eyes.

Tony was sitting on the floor beside Jackie (I noticed he'd carefully placed himself on a cushion so as not to get his precious white trousers dirty), holding one of Jackie's shoes. She was looking up at him, smiling, obviously delighted to have his attention, but equally obviously she hadn't got a clue about what he was trying to make her do.

'I thought you said she'd understand.' Tony looked up, frowning, and he sounded disappointed. 'I've been telling her to put her shoe on for the last five minutes, and she won't do it.'

'Yes, but it's like telling someone to make a cake without giving them the recipe,' I said. 'You've got to show her bit by bit.'

I sat down too, and he gave me the shoe. Then I put it into Jackie's hands and guided it on to her foot. She laughed. It was another lovely new game to her. As soon as I took my hands away, she dropped hers too, and the shoe fell to the floor.

Tony was ready to give up.

'She'll never do it,' he said.

'Yes she will.' I was sure of Jackie now that she'd been so clever with her hair. 'Wait and see. We'll do this every day, a few minutes at a time, and she'll get the idea in the end. She can't concentrate for long. It was much harder, getting her to do her hair. You know what, by the time your mum finishes her course, I'm going to have Jackie doing all sorts of things. I'm going to surprise her with it. Don't let on, will you?'

We both got to our feet. Jackie was already standing by the door, ready to go out.

'Just a minute,' I said. 'You haven't been on the potty yet.'

She squirmed between my legs, and made for the bathroom. Tony was going in the same direction. I knew he'd be in there for hours, fussing over his hair and gazing at himself in the mirror.

'One day,' I thought, 'I'm going to introduce you to Debbie. You'd suit each other down to the ground.' But out loud I said, 'Do you mind if we go in first? Jackie will never be able to wait until you've finished.'

He laughed. It was funny but I was really getting to like Tony, in a sisterish kind of way.

Outside, the weather had turned. The clouds had blown away, and the sun was out. I was fed up with our usual walk, down to the park and into the playground. On an impulse, I turned the pushchair and began the long climb up the hill towards the church.

I was puffed when I got to the top. I'd have made Jackie walk if she'd been mine. It would have done her good. But Mrs Maynard was neurotic about roads, and I must say, she did have reason to be. Jackie didn't have the faintest idea about danger. She'd have run in front of a ten-ton truck without a moment's thought.

It was a while since I'd been to church, so I felt a bit embarrassed when Mr Henderson popped out of the vestry door and practically bumped into me. I hadn't expected to see him there.

'Hi, Anna!' He bent down, and poked Jackie in the tummy. 'Hey! Who are you?'

'She's Jackie.' I felt suddenly proud of her. 'I'm looking after her.'

'Good for you,' he said. I could see he was thinking of saying something embarrassing, about Ben, or about me being specially fit for this kind of job, but he didn't say anything. Mr Henderson could be very tactful.

'We've missed you at the club,' he said.

'I'm sorry . . .' I began in a rush, feeling around for an excuse and not finding one.

'Don't be sorry.' He interrupted me with a smile. 'Just come on Friday. They've organized a disco. "Over my dead body," I said, but they insisted. Jeff asked me what had happened to you.'

'Are you sure he meant me?' I asked. I didn't want to be had twice.

'Well, he said "Anna Peacock", and asked for your phone number. I gave it to him. I hope you don't mind. He said he'd call you this evening.'

I couldn't help it, but I got that daft sort of kick in the stomach feeling again.

'You idiot,' I told myself sternly. 'You only stopped thinking about Tony yesterday.' But I knew it wasn't a question of love. It was more a feeling of something exciting about to happen, and a new, more confident me, a hundred years older than I'd been a year ago. A thousand times wiser.

'Mustn't hold you up,' said Mr Henderson, opening the door of the graveyard for the pushchair. 'I suppose you've come to visit Ben's grave.'

I hadn't, but I went in anyway. It was the first time I'd dared come since the funeral. I don't know why, but I hadn't wanted to. The idea of it had sort of turned me up. Mum came regularly, I knew, and tidied it up, and planted flowers and things. But I'd always made an excuse not to go with her.

It took me a minute or two to find it, but there it was at last, under an old oak tree in the corner of the cemetery. The stone said simply:

Benedict Peacock
Aged 2 years

A ripple of wind ran through the long grass at the edge of the field beyond the hedge, and ruffled the leaves. It blew Jackie's scarf across her face, and she wriggled to be let out of the pushchair. I undid the strap and she struggled free, then, feeling playful after being held down for so long, she started to run round, peering out at me from behind the grave stones, clambering on to chunks of granite and sliding clumsily off them again, pointing and laughing at marble angels.

'No Jackie,' I started to say, 'not here.' It seemed disrespectful to the dead somehow, to use the graveyard as a playground. But then I thought of Ben in my dream, swimming free and happy, strong and supple, away into the middle of the lake, and I let her play. Ben wouldn't have minded, I was quite sure of that. He'd have tried to follow her, getting his dungarees muddy, and laughing every time she whisked her sweet little face around to wave at him.

Also by Elizabeth Laird

Dindy
and the
Elephant

Turn the page to read an extract . . .

Chapter One

'Let's play Going to England,' said Pog.

Pog's my little brother. His real name's Derek, but everyone calls him Pog. Don't ask me why. (My real name's Margaret, but everyone calls me Dindy.)

'It's silly to play Going to England,' I said. 'It's horrible there. All bombsites and rationing and fog.'

'But I *want* to,' said Pog, pushing out his lower lip in the annoying way he does when he's about to cry.

I might as well explain straight away that we live in India, in the middle of a tea plantation. Our bungalow is on a little hill with tea bushes spreading away from it all around, and jungle on the hilltops above. The nearest town is Munnar, which takes ages to get to, even on Daddy's motorbike, and our nearest English neighbours are the Richardsons, who are on the next plantation miles away. So Pog and I are on our own all the time. There's no school for British children, so Mother does our lessons at home, when she feels like it, which is hardly ever.

Pog and I had played Going to England so many times that I was fed up with it. I was nine after all, and a bit old for Let's Pretend. So I looked around, trying to think of something else to do.

Mother was resting and didn't want to be disturbed, Krishna the cook was in a bad mood as usual and would have chased us out of the kitchen, and Shanti, our ayah, who had looked after us since we were born, had gone to Munnar to get some things for Mother.

Pog was looking at me with big eyes. Once he'd thought of playing Going to England, I knew he'd go on and on about it until I gave in. All he wanted to do was wobble about pretending to walk up the gangway on to the ship, and go 'ooh' and 'ah' while he watched the bit of water between the ship and dock get wider and wider. After that, he'd spend ages marching up and down being the ship's captain and giving orders to the crew (me).

What Pog didn't know was that I thought about going to England all the time. Not to pretend. For real.

One of the main things about me is that I'm good at keeping still and being quiet. Grown-ups often think

I'm not listening when they talk. But I *do*. And I hear things.

A week earlier, I'd overheard a conversation that had really made me worried.

It was just an ordinary evening except that Dr Dysart had come over for dinner. I liked Dr Dysart. He was always kind, even when he had to do awful things like cutting your tonsils out. He talked in a drawly, Scottish kind of voice. Daddy's got a Scottish accent too, because he comes from Glasgow.

I was sitting on the window seat, as out of sight as possible, with my legs curled up under me, pretending to read *The Secret Garden* but really watching everyone out of the corner of my eye and listening as hard as I could.

'The Indians will have us out of India as soon as they can,' I heard Daddy say. 'They're talking about independence everywhere. Riots, demonstrations – they'll get their way. Soon too.'

Mother's face went red. She held out her glass and shook it to make Sunderam (that's the name of our bearer) fill it up again with gin. I hate it when Mother drinks too much. She goes stupid and giggly, and then she gets cross.

'Oh, Frank,' she said, hitching up the shoulder

strap of her pink satin evening gown. 'Don't be silly. If the British leave India, everything will just fall apart. You know what children the natives are.'

I looked at Sunderam's face and saw it close up. I knew what he thought of Mother. I'd often heard him and Krishna talk about her when they forgot to close the kitchen door. Pog and I can understand everything the servants say to each other. Shanti taught us their language (Malayalam) before we could even speak English.

Dr Dysart put the tips of his fingers together and looked up at the ceiling.

'I don't like to contradict you, dear lady,' he said, 'but India will do very well without the British. My own colleague, Kumar, to take one example, is an excellent doctor. Rather impressive, as a matter of fact.'

Mother's face went even redder.

'Impressive? What on earth do you mean? Native doctors are all the same. Nothing but herbs and leaves and mumbo-jumbo.'

Dr Dysart frowned.

'Dr Kumar trained in Edinburgh, and he's better qualified than I am. A fine surgeon too.' He picked up his glass and took a gulp of whisky. 'Which brings me to my own bit of news. I'm pulling out,

I'm afraid. Leaving India for good. The old ticker's been playing up for a while and a quiet retirement near my daughter in Stirling is what's in store for me.'

Daddy put his own drink down on the little table beside his chair so sharply that I thought he'd cracked the glass.

'Dysart! My dear fellow! I had no idea you had a heart condition. Not too serious, I hope?'

'But you can't go, Dr Dysart! You can't!' Mother was almost shouting. 'You can't leave us here without you! How will I manage? You're the only person who understands my headaches, my spasms, my sleepless nights . . .'

I wasn't sure, but I thought that Dr Dysart was trying not to smile.

'There's nothing seriously wrong with you, Daphne, as I've told you many times. A little less gin, a little healthy exercise, some useful activity . . .'

'They'll be replacing you, I suppose?' said Daddy.

'Yes, of course.' Dr Dysart looked up at the ceiling again. 'Dr Kumar is taking over my practice. From next week, actually. He's a remarkable young man. I have every confidence in him.'

'An Indian? I wouldn't let him near me!' Mother almost shrieked. 'Frank, what are we going to do? Frank!'

Daddy shoved his chair back, scraping it noisily on the tiled floor as he stood up.

'We're going to have dinner,' he said shortly. 'Surely it's ready by now?' He turned to look at Sunderam, who was standing by the door, and was so still that he looked as if he'd been stuffed. 'Go and hurry them up in the kitchen, will you?'

Then he noticed me.

'Margaret! Why are you still up? Go and find Shanti and get her to put you to bed at once.'

I swung my legs off the window seat and went slowly towards the door, but as I opened it I heard Dr Dysart say, 'What about you and Daphne, Frank? Are you staying on? It'll be different here once the British leave. Have you thought of Kenya? I hear they're expanding the tea plantations in East Africa now.'

And Daddy said gloomily, 'No, it'll have to be England. It's time the bairns were at school. I'd try sheep farming in New Zealand, but Daphne wants London.'

As I went out, I heard Mother say crossly, 'Of course I do. After this ghastly place, I want a bit of *life*. Especially now we're being *abandoned* by our friends. I've persuaded Frank to start making enquiries at last.'

I shut the door as loudly as I dared.